Mahoney was the first over the barricade, bellowing like an elephant, enraged at the Germans for shooting him in the leg.

"KILL THE BASTARDS!" Mahoney screamed

Immediately a German parried Mahoney's bayonet to the side and tried to slam him in the head with his rifle butt, but Mahoney ducked and brought his own rifle butt straight up, catching the German on the chin. As the German fell backwards, Mahoney brought his bayonet down and slashed the German from neck to hip bone.

Mahoney sidestepped another and spun around and found himself face to face with an American soldier. They made a motion to charge each other, realized they were on the same side, grinned, and turned to look for more Germans to kill....

Bantam Books by Gordon Davis
Ask your bookseller for the books you have missed

THE LIBERATION OF PARIS—THE SERGEANT #4
DOOM RIVER—THE SERGEANT #5
SLAUGHTER CITY—THE SERGEANT #6
BULLET BRIDGE—THE SERGEANT #7
BLOODY BASTOGNE—THE SERGEANT #8

THE SERGEANT # 8
BLOODY BASTOGNE

Gordon Davis

BANTAM BOOKS
TORONTO · NEW YORK · LONDON · SYDNEY

BLOODY BASTOGNE: THE SERGEANT #8
A Bantam Book / December 1981

Created by Walter Zacharius

All rights reserved.
Copyright © 1981 by Kensington Publishing Corp.
Cover art copyright © 1981 by Bantam Books, Inc.
This book may not be reproduced in whole or in part, by mimeograph or any other means, without permission.
For information address: Bantam Books, Inc.

ISBN 0-553-20034-8

Published simultaneously in the United States and Canada

Bantam Books are published by Bantam Books, Inc. Its trademark, consisting of the words "Bantam Books" and the portrayal of a rooster, is Registered in U.S. Patent and Trademark Office and in other countries. Marca Registrada. Bantam Books, Inc., 666 Fifth Avenue, New York, New York 10103.

PRINTED IN THE UNITED STATES OF AMERICA

0 9 8 7 6 5 4 3 2 1

ONE

A light snow fell on the little Belgian town of Clervaux, near the border of Germany. It was night, and a lone jeep turned a corner in a secluded neighborhood. Light streamed from the window of a café halfway up the street.

"That must be the joint," said Master Sergeant C. J. Mahoney, sitting behind the wheel and pointing with a finger of his big glove.

"Must be," replied Master Sergeant Frank Hooper, sitting next to him and puffing a cigarette.

Several jeeps, two deuce and a half trucks, and one Sherman tank were parked along the street. Mahoney steered his jeep into the space behind the Sherman tank, stopped but did not pull up the emergency brake because it could freeze in the cold night air.

Mahoney turned off the engine, unbuttoned his thick wool overcoat, and took out a cigar, biting off the end and placing the cigar in his mouth. He lit it with his Zippo and took a few puffs to make sure it was burning well. Hooper opened the door of the jeep and stepped into the snow.

"Colder than a well-digger's ass," Hooper muttered, his breath making clouds of condensation.

Mahoney got out of the jeep and turned up his collar. He wore a knitted GI visored cap underneath his steel helmet, and a Colt .45 was strapped to his waist. He trudged through the snow to the other side of the jeep and joined Hooper. Together they walked toward the café.

They were tall husky men, clean-shaven because they'd heard that whores could be found in the café ahead. Mahoney was the taller and better looking of the two, despite a scar on his cheek and a nose that had been broken once and reset a bit out of line. Hooper was wider and heavier, and his face looked like the front end of a bulldozer.

The falling snow made luminous halos around the street lamps, and the front window of the café glowed golden. Already Mahoney could hear the tinkle of a piano and the sound of men's and women's voices. His step quickened as he thought of beautiful women smelling of fancy perfume, laughing and offering glimpses of their thighs whenever they crossed their legs.

They stopped in front of the café and looked through the window. The glass was covered with ice and mist, but soldiers in o.d. green and women in bright-colored dresses could be dimly perceived.

"Hot dog!" said Hooper with a maniacal grin, reaching for the doorknob.

He opened the door, and Mahoney followed him into the bistro. It was filled with tobacco smoke, and a civilian sat at the piano in a corner, pounding the keys. Near him some GIs and women were singing. The GIs wore the Ivy Leaf patch of the Fourth Division, and some of them looked curiously at Mahoney and Hooper as they made their way to the bar. Mahoney and Hooper wore the black hammer of the Thirty-third Division, known as the Hammerheads, which was part of Patton's Third Army farther south. They and a handful of other Third Army men had been sent on a reconnaissance mission into the Ardennes sector, which was protecting the Third Army's right flank, and Patton wanted to know if it was as weakly defended as he'd heard. Mahoney and the rest of the Third Army recon team had confirmed Patton's suspicions, relayed the information to his headquarters, and would return to their units in a day or two.

Mahoney and Hooper stepped up to the bar, unbuttoning their heavy woolen overcoats. They placed their helmets on the bar but left their knitted caps on. The bartender, a roly-poly bald man with a curled up mustache, waddled toward them. He was smiling happily because he was making piles of money from the GIs.

"Got any whisky?" Mahoney asked.

"Only wine, beer, and brandy."

"Two brandies—for me and my father here."

The bartender poured the drinks as Mahoney looked around.

GIs from the Fourth Division lined the bar and sat at the tables, talking with women of all sizes and shapes, from their late teens or early twenties to their late forties.

"Lookit all the cunt!" Hooper said, grabbing his glass.

Hooper was more concerned with raw sex than with aesthetics and searched the room for an old babe whom he might take to one of the back rooms immediately.

He saw a heavily made up blonde sitting at a table in the corner with a drunken GI who wore glasses crooked on his nose and looked like a company clerk. The whore had a big bust and appeared bored. Hooper knew from experience that whores her age usually knew how to give exotic blowjobs, and that was exactly what he'd come here for.

He pointed with his chin toward the whore. "Looka there," he said to Mahoney.

"Where?"

"The blonde in the corner."

Mahoney had become accustomed to Hooper's taste in the few days they'd been together and spotted her instantly. "She's real nice," Mahoney said. "Why don't you go over there and tell her how wonderful you are."

"I'm on my way," Hooper said, placing his helmet under his arm and lifting his glass off the bar.

Hooper swaggered confidently toward the blonde whore, who looked up at him and smiled when she saw him approaching. She figured that although he wasn't very good-looking, he wore sergeant's stripes and probably had more money than the Pfc with his arm around her shoulder. The whore hit the Pfc in the ribs with her elbow, and he slid off his chair, collapsing onto the floor. Hooper grinned as he sat down in the scarecrow's chair, placing his arm around the whore's shoulders. The whore beamed because she thought she'd finally found herself a winner.

Mahoney leaned his back against the bar and swallowed another gulp of brandy. He knew it was much easier to get along with women if you weren't particular, but he'd always liked beautiful women and always went for the best looking one in his vicinity. There'd been times when he'd had to settle for whores like the one Hooper was beginning to paw, but that had only been after he'd exhausted all the other possibilities.

He scanned the room back and forth, wondering which

whore to pick, when the back door opened and a young corporal entered the room, followed by a brunette in her early twenties. The brunette had shoulder length hair and lovely lips. Her figure was understated rather than voluptuous, and her legs appeared shapely. Mahoney considered her the best looking whore in the joint.

The corporal blushed and smiled sheepishly as his drunken buddies at a nearby table applauded him. The piano player continued to pound out the same song and the crowd of drunks nearby tried to sing along. The corporal said something to the whore, but she shook her head and walked toward the bar. Her face was expressionless, but her eyes spoke of boredom and resignation. She stopped at the bar and asked the bartender for a cup of coffee. Seconds later, Mahoney squeezed in beside her.

"Hi," he said with a smile.

She looked up at him because she was five foot six and he was six foot four. "I'm taking a break," she said. "Maybe you'd better find another girl."

"There's nobody else that I want."

She shrugged and smiled, then turned away from him as the bartender placed a cup of black coffee in front of her. She gazed into it as if it contained the answers to all her questions. She touched the handle of the cup, and Mahoney admired her small delicate hand. She'd probably just blown that corporal, but she looked lovely anyway. Mahoney felt an ache in his heart when he thought this young woman had to screw the troops in order to stay alive. He could sense her despair and the tragedy of her life because he'd known despair and tragedy too. He'd been in the war since the first landings in North Africa, had been wounded many times, and many of his closest friends had been killed in action.

"I'll pay you just to talk with me," he said. "We don't have to go back there if you don't want to."

She looked sideways at him for a few moments. "I'm not a very good talker," she said. "I still think you ought to find another girl."

"I don't want another girl." He placed five bucks on the bar.

She thought for a few moments, then covered the money with her tiny hand.

He picked up her cup of coffee and his glass of brandy, carrying them through the cigarette smoke to a table for two against the far wall. It had a candle burning inside a holder that had once been a bottle of cheap wine, and there was a dirty tin ashtray half-filled with butts. The piano player switched to a boogie-woogie tune.

Mahoney and the girl sat at the table. She took a cigarette out of her pocketbook, and he held out the flame from his Zippo. She puffed the cigarette to life while scrutinizing his face. Mahoney wondered what she saw. Whenever a woman looked at him that way, he was afraid he wouldn't measure up. Despite all his romantic conquests of the past, the only woman who really mattered was the one he was with at the moment.

"You from around here?" Mahoney asked.

"No," she replied, sipping her coffee.

"Where are you from?"

"Somewhere."

Mahoney realized she didn't want him to know. Most whores were as secretive as espionage agents in enemy territory. "What's your name?"

"Madeleine."

"I'm Mahoney."

"Why do you have a different insignia on your shoulder than the other soldiers here?"

"I'm from an outfit farther south, and I'm up here on temporary duty."

She inhaled her cigarette and blew the smoke through pursed lips. Mahoney felt awkward because he didn't know what to say to her. She was tried and evidently didn't have the energy to make conversation.

"I'm sorry," he said. "I guess I'm being a pain in the neck."

She examined him again and puffed her cigarette. "That's all right. It's my fault. I should be more entertaining, I suppose, but I'm awfully tired."

"Don't worry about it. You're pretty, and it's nice to just sit here with you. You may not feel so well, but you're making me feel better."

She smiled. "You're sweet. After I finish this cup of coffee we can go in back."

Mahoney sipped his brandy and looked at her. He was amazed by how attractive she was, but he knew she wouldn't stay this way long. A few years of screwing the troops, and she'd look like a hag. He wanted to tell her to find some other line of work, but she'd probably tried and couldn't.

"You look sad," she said. "What's wrong?"

"Nothing."

"Thinking about your girl back home?"

"I don't have a girl back home."

"No? A handsome soldier like you? I don't believe you."

"It's the truth. I don't."

"Why not?"

"Who the hell knows?"

"You mustn't have tried very hard."

He shrugged. "Maybe I never found anybody worth the effort. Anyway, I move around a lot, and it's hard to get romances going when you're always leaving for someplace else."

"Yes," she said, "I suppose a soldier's life is very difficult."

"I don't think it's any more difficult than yours."

She sighed. "Well, the war will end one day, and then life will return to normal."

"Sometimes I think the war will never end," he said. "Sometimes I think it'll go on forever."

"Don't say that. I don't think I could bear it."

He looked into her eyes. "You know, the longer I sit with you, the lovelier you become. I think I could fall in love with somebody like you. You'd definitely be worth the effort."

She smiled. "You probably haven't seen any women for a long time. That's why you're saying that."

"No, it's true. It's hard to say why one person is attracted to another person, but you ring all my bells, kiddo."

She lifted her cup of coffee to her lips. "Don't talk like that because I'm liable to believe you."

"I want you to believe me."

"What for? You don't have to tell me stories. I've heard a million of them."

He placed his hand on hers. "I'm just telling you the way I feel. You may not like it, but it's the truth."

"The truth?" She made a sarcastic expression. "I know why you're talking this way. You just want me to give you a better time back there, but don't worry, you'll get your money's worth."

"Lady," Mahoney said, "if you just laid still with your eyes closed, I'd have a good time."

She looked at him, and her eyes softened. She touched the palm of her hand to his cheek. "You know, you're awfully nice. I don't know why I'm arguing with you. I suppose if we had met under normal circumstances, I might have fallen in love with you too. You're very good-looking, and you have a nice way about you."

Like the tentacle of an octopus, an arm dropped down out of the smoke and grabbed Madeleine's arm.

"Hiya baby," said a big staff sergeant with a head like an artillery shell. "Remember me?"

She wrinkled her nose and looked up at him. "You're hurting my arm."

The staff sergeant loosened his grip a little. "Let's go fickey-fick in the back room, baby."

"I'm busy."

The sergeant chortled. "The whole world's busy. Let's go."

Mahoney stood up. "Take your hands off her."

The sergeant looked at Mahoney and scowled. He had tiny pig eyes and a mouth full of big teeth. "Stay out of this if you know what's good for you."

"I said, take your fucking hands off her."

The menace in Mahoney's voice was unmistakable. The sergeant knew that Mahoney meant business. He looked Mahoney up and down. Mahoney was taller than he, but he had more body weight. Soldiers at nearby tables were looking, and the sergeant couldn't back down.

"Who's gonna make me take my hands off her?" the sergeant asked.

Mahoney brought his left fist up from the table in a movement so fast it was a blur. His fist slammed against the sergeant's jaw and lifted him off his feet. The sergeant went flying through the air and landed on his back in the middle of a big round table. The girls sitting at the table shrieked and jumped backwards, and the men got out of the way. Mahoney dived onto the sergeant, grabbed him by the neck, and prepared to bash his head against the table.

The sergeant reared back his right fist and walloped Mahoney on the mouth. Mahoney saw stars, let go the sergeant's neck, and wobbled to the side. The sergeant hit Mahoney again, and Mahoney sagged off him, falling from the table and landing stomach down on the floor. The sergeant lunged at him, but Mahoney rolled out of the way and jumped to his feet.

The sergeant got up and glowered at Mahoney. Girls screamed, and the Fourth Division soldiers cheered for the sergeant, whom many evidently knew. The bartender tried to get through to break up the fight, but the Fourth Division men wouldn't let him pass.

The sergeant wiped a trickle of blood from the corner of his mouth and looked at it. "You fucking cocksucker!" he snarled at Mahoney.

Mahoney motioned with his hand. "C'mon," he said, "any time you feel froggy, just go ahead and jump."

The sergeant reached into his pocket and came out with a switchblade knife. He hit the button and the four inch blade snapped out and gleamed in the light from the candles. He sliced the air a few times with the blade and then advanced sideways toward Mahoney.

The sergeant bared his teeth at Mahoney. "I'm gonna cut your fucking ass off," he said.

Mahoney saw a bottle of wine sitting atop a nearby table. He rushed toward it, lifted it by the neck, and smashed it down on the edge of the table. Wine and shards of glass splattered in all directions, and Mahoney turned to the sergeant, waving the broken edge back and forth. "You're gonna eat this fucking bottle—*that's* what you're gonna do," Mahoney replied.

The two men circled each other as the soldiers and whores held their breaths. Mahoney and the sergeant feinted toward each other and drew back, concentrating completely, looking for an opening.

Hooper came out of the back room with his blonde whore and saw the crowd. He dragged the whore behind him and pushed his way through, his jaw dropping open when he saw

Mahoney with the broken bottle facing the staff sergeant with a big knife.

The sergeant tried to smile and show confidence, as sweat made rivulets on his forehead and dripped down his cheeks. He rocked from heel to heel, flicking his knife through the air, knowing that a false move could cost him his life.

Mahoney held his broken bottle steady, his eyes fixed on the switchblade. His chin was tucked into his throat, and he held his left arm at stomach level to block any slashes that came that way. The café was so quiet you could hear water dripping in the sink.

Hooper pushed his way into the circle and grinned. "Hey you guys—why don't you shake hands and make up before you get in trouble?"

The sergeant from the Fourth Division snarled at him, "Mind your own business, Fatso!"

Mahoney kept his eyes on the switchblade. "Stay outta this, Hooper."

Hooper stepped back into the crowd. He wanted to call the MPs before somebody got hurt, but if he called the MPs, Mahoney would go to the stockade.

The sergeant leaned toward Mahoney, who balanced himself on the balls of his feet. Their eyes met and hatred passed between them like high voltage current. Mahoney opened his lips and spoke through teeth on edge. "C'mon, fuckhead," he said.

The sergeant went *oof* and lunged forward, streaking his knife toward Mahoney's face. Mahoney stepped to the side and pushed the edge of the broken bottle into the sergeant's wrist, slashing all the way up his arm. The sergeant screamed and jumped back, but Mahoney kept after him. Mahoney ripped the bottle across the sergeant's face, nearly slicing off his nose, and the sergeant bellowed as he whipped his knife wildly through the air. Mahoney grabbed the sergeant's wrist with his left hand and dug the broken bottle into the sergeant's belly, twisting it around. The sergeant continued to scream as blood poured from his arm, face, and stomach. He tried to break loose from Mahoney's iron grip, but Mahoney wouldn't let him go. He tried to kick Mahoney in the balls, but Mahoney stepped to the side and slashed sideways with the bottle, ripping apart the sergeant's windpipe.

Blood gurgled out of the sergeant's mouth, and he went limp, dropping to his knees on the floor. He held both his hands to his throat, trying to stanch the blood, looking up at Mahoney pleadingly. Then he pitched forward onto his face as whistles blew and MPs charged into the little café.

TWO

Twenty miles west of Clervaux, in Bastogne, Belgium, Major General Troy Middleton, commander of the Eighth Corps, was uneasy. He paced back and forth in his office, looking nervously at the maps strewn over his table. Reports had been coming in all evening about movements of heavy armor behind the German lines. A woman had been sent up from the Twenty-eighth Division earlier in the afternoon, and she said she'd seen huge formations of German troops behind the Siegfried Line east of Clervaux. Middleton had sent her to First Army headquarters in Spa, but staff officers there believed the German troops were only training in the area. The enemy used that sector as a rest and training area, as did the First Army.

General Middleton hoped the staff officers at First Army were right because if the Germans attacked through his area, a massacre of American soldiers was likely to ensue. The Ardennes sector was the weakest part of the American line, the so-called "Ghost Front," where nothing ever happened and artillery was fired mainly for registration. American and German soldiers waved to each other across no-man's-land, and sometimes they got close enough to chit-chat. Reports had been received that American and German soldiers even engaged in black market activities with each other.

Middleton had only six under-strength divisions holding a ninety mile front. Three of the divisions were green and had been sent to the area to get "blooded" before being transferred to sectors where the real war was taking place. The other three divisions, which included the famous Fourth Division, were recuperating from the bloody Hurtgen Forest campaign, where tremendous losses had been suffered.

Middleton was a heavyset man who wore glasses and had a hook nose. He'd been dean of administration at Louisiana State University before being recalled to active duty at the beginning of the war. Prior to that, he'd served twenty-seven years in the Army and had been a colonel of infantry in the First World War.

Middleton looked down at the map and adjusted his wire-rimmed glasses on his nose. General Bradley at EAGLE TAC and General Hodges at First Army had told him that the Germans would never attack through the Ardennes although they'd come this way in 1940 when they had attacked France. General Bradley said that if the Germans were foolish enough to attack, General Hodges would hit them in flank from the north and General Patton would do the same in the south, catching them in the jaws of a giant American nutcracker.

But Middleton knew it would take several days for that nutcracker to get moving, and by then, the Germans might very well roll over his men and his own headquarters in Bastogne.

Well, he thought, scratching his jaw, I hope to hell they really are on maneuvers over there.

The Fourth Division MPs roughed up Mahoney a little in the back of the three-quarter ton truck as it drove through the streets of Clervaux on the way to the Provost Marshal's office. Mahoney's hands were handcuffed behind his back, but he could take a punch pretty well, and he rolled with them as the MPs batted him around. He was from a strange division, and he'd made them leave their warm headquarters. He'd nearly killed one of their own, and they were going to make him pay for it.

The truck stopped in front of the Provost Marshal's office, and the MPs let down the tailgate. They dragged Mahoney out, and he fell to his knees in the snow. He shook his head and tried to clear out the fog, wishing he didn't have the cuffs on because he'd love to wade into the MPs and bust a few heads.

They picked him up and pulled him into the big building

that was the MP headquarters in Clervaux. An old MP master sergeant with white hair sat behind the high desk and looked down as the other MPs held Mahoney's arms.

"He went at a guy with a bottle," one of the MPs said. "The guy might die."

Mahoney cleared his throat. "He pulled a knife on me first."

An MP elbowed him in the ribs. "Speak when you're spoken to, shit-for-brains!"

Mahoney looked up at the old master sergeant. If this had happened in the Hammerhead Division, they'd probably have known each other because Mahoney knew everybody of consequence in the division. But here he was like an orphan.

"What's your name?" the old master sergeant asked.

Mahoney told him.

"What're you doing here?"

"I'm on TDY with First Army."

"From where?"

"Third Army."

The old sergeant squinted his eyes. "Is that the Hammerhead patch I see on your shoulder there?"

"Yeah."

The MP elbowed him in the ribs again. "Say *yes, Sergeant*."

"Yes, Sergeant."

The old sergeant sneered. "You Hammerheads are supposed to be a real fancy bunch of soldiers."

Mahoney didn't reply. The MP hit him a shot in the ribs again, and it doubled Mahoney over.

"He asked you a question, scumbag!" the MP said.

Slowly Mahoney straightened up and glowered at the MP, who had swarthy skin and looked Italian.

"If I ever see you outside this stockade," Mahoney said through bloody lips, "I'm going to fucking kill you."

"WHAT!"

The MPs attacked him and beat him to the floor with clubs and fists until he was unconscious.

"Lock him up," the old master sergeant said.

The MPs grabbed Mahoney's clothes and dragged him across the floor toward the cells.

* * *

Less than three hundred miles away, on the German side of the Siegfried Line, Adolph Hitler was chatting with Martin Bormann, the head of the Nazi Party Chancery, and with Walther Hewell, a diplomatic liaison officer with the Foreign Service, in the Eagle's Nest, Hitler's headquarters near the Western Front.

Hitler was in an unusually ebullient mood despite the recent throat operation that prevented him from speaking loudly. In a hoarse whisper, he lectured Bormann and Hewell on the lessons of History.

"Frederick II earned his title *the Great*," Hitler explained, "not just because he was victorious, but because he did not despair in adversity. In the same manner, History will come to recognize me because I too will never have surrendered after grievous misfortunes."

Bormann and Hewell listened to Hitler with rapt attention, their eyes glistening with devotion. They did not try to speak because they didn't want to miss any of their Fuehrer's precious words.

"This war," Hitler continued, "will determine the survival or extinction of the German people. It demands the unqualified commitment of every individual. Even seemingly hopeless situations have been mastered by the blind courage and bravery of our soldiers, the stubborn steadfastness of all ranks, and my calm unyielding leadership."

Hitler sat on a sofa in front of a low table on which was a glass of mineral water. He looked over the heads of Bormann and Hewell at the huge oil portrait of himself on the wall. It had been painted in the early thirties and showed him wearing a brown shirt, a resolute expression on his face and a dagger at his waist. At one time he used to give small autographed copies of the painting to his female admirers, but there was no time for that anymore.

"I would like you gentlemen to leave me now," Hitler said. "I need some time to think."

"Yes, sir!" they said in unison, jumping to their feet. They saluted, shouted "Heil Hitler!" and marched out of the room, closing the door behind them.

Alone, Hitler raised the glass of mineral water to his lips and drank some down. He believed the mineral water was good for him, along with his health food vegetarian diet, although he suffered from terrible stomach cramps, headaches, flatulence, and numerous other ailments.

He wanted to savor these final hours alone, for it was nearly one o'clock on the morning of December 16th, and his long awaited and carefully planned Ardennes Offensive, codenamed Operation *Wacht am Rhein,* was scheduled to begin in only four and a half hours.

He and his staff had been planning this operation since early September. They'd managed to draw together a quarter of a million soldiers, 970 tanks, 1,900 pieces of heavy artillery, 3.8 million gallons of gasoline, and 50 trainloads of ammunition on the German side of the Siegfried Line. Also there were 350 new planes, among them 80 of the latest jets.

At five-thirty they'd strike into the Ardennes and roll over the scanty American positions. Utilizing tried and proven blitzkrieg techniques, they'd knife through Belgium, cross the Meuse River, and continue on to Antwerp, capturing the big allied port there and splitting the British and American armies in half. Then they'd annihilate the British Army, knock the Americans senseless, and transfer the bulk of the forces back to the Eastern front, where they'd attack relentlessly until they brought Stalin to his knees.

Hitler knew very well that the fate of the Third Reich was riding on Operation *Wacht am Rhein,* but he was confident he'd win the great victory that he so ardently desired. However, many of his leading generals, among them von Rundstedt and Model, believed they didn't have enough men and material to attain all the operation's strategic objectives, though Hitler had been right and they'd been wrong many times in the past. Surely it would be that way again.

Hitler chuckled to himself. The Allies thought they had him nearly defeated, but he'd show them a thing or two during the next few days. The fools wouldn't know what had hit them.

THREE

Mahoney awoke on the cold stone floor of his cell in the MP station in Clervaux. His head felt as though it had been run over by the Red Ball Express, and he ached all over his body. He had difficulty opening his mouth, because his lips were sealed by dried blood. Moistening the blood with his wetted tongue, he pulled his lips apart and opened his mouth. He touched his teeth with his tongue; some of them were loose.

"Those fucking bastards," he muttered, getting up and sitting heavily on the wooden cot affixed to the wall. He felt his ribs and bones to discover whether anything was broken, but it appeared that nothing was. The MPs had jabbed him in the gut with their billy clubs, and he might be pissing blood for awhile, but those were the breaks of the game.

He wished he had a cigarette, but the bastards had taken all of them away from him. Glancing at his watch to find out the time, he saw that they'd taken that away too. He cursed them again and shivered in the cold cell. His overcoat had been left behind in the café, and he wore only a fatigue shirt with a wool sweater underneath it. He realized he was in a serious mess.

If this had happened in the Third Army, he'd probably be free as a bird right now, but he was in hostile territory, even if it was held by the same U.S. Army that he was in. Hooper would testify that the other guy pulled a knife first, but who knew where Hooper was, and there might not be a trial anyway. They might just take him out back and shoot him down. Afterwards, they'd say he'd tried to escape. Such things happened from time to time in the Army.

And it was all because of a piece of ass, from a whore of all things, and he didn't even get into her pants. He closed his eyes and remembered her sitting at the table, holding her coffee cup with dainty fingers, her face as pretty as any movie star's. Naw, he thought, she's not really a whore, and she's not just another piece of ass either. She'd touched his heart somehow in the brief time they'd been together, and he hoped he'd see her again someday. He was glad he'd kept that sergeant away from her. Mahoney wondered if he'd died. Fuck him anyway.

He heard a commotion in another part of the jail. Somebody was shouting in German, "The Germans are coming tonight, I tell you! Why don't you believe me?"

"Shaddup, kraut!" said an American voice, and Mahoney heard something that sounded like a punch in the mouth.

The commotion came closer, and Mahoney saw a group of MPs dragging a German soldier through the corridor. The German's blond head hung down, and Mahoney realized that the MPs must have really clobbered him. They passed Mahoney and opened a cell farther down the corridor. Mahoney pushed his head against the bars of his cell and could see the MPs throwing the German soldier into a cell.

The MPs walked toward Mahoney, and he held out his hand. "How about a cigarette, boys?"

"Fuck you," replied one of the MPs.

"Hey—c'mon," Mahoney said. "We're in the same Army, aren't we?"

Another MP stopped and reached toward his shirt pocket. "I can't deny a man a cigarette," he said in a Southern drawl.

"Don't get too close to him!"

"He don't look so dangerous to me."

The MP held out a cigarette, and Mahoney took it, placing it between his bloody lips as the other MPs watched glumly. The first MP held out his Zippo and flicked the wheel, bringing the fire close to the cigarette. Mahoney puffed and filled his lungs with the rich smoke.

"Thanks, buddy," Mahoney said.

The MP winked.

"What's with the kraut?"

"He's a deserter. We picked him up tonight."

"He said the Germans are going to attack."

The MP cocked an eye. "How you know that?"

"I speak kraut."

"Yeah, that's what he told the officer who interrogated him. The information's been sent up to Corps."

"Let's go!" said one of the other MPs.

The MP who'd given Mahoney the light moved off into the darkness with the others. Mahoney sat on his cot and puffed the cigarette, feeling better already. Everybody always said that cigarettes were bad for you and cut your wind, but how could they be so bad if they always made you feel better? He thought of the German and wondered if he was telling the truth about the attack or whether he was just a nut or if he'd been sent by the Germans to confuse everybody. The Germans were tricky people, and you never knew what they could be up to.

Down the corridor, the German muttered to himself. Mahoney arose from his cot and stepped toward the bars of his cell. He'd learned to speak German fluently when he was in North Africa, dealing black market goods to the Germans in the big POW camp near Oran.

"How are you feeling?" Mahoney called down the corridor in German.

There was a pause, and then the German soldier replied, "Who's there?"

"An American soldier behind bars like you."

"You speak German!"

"What'd you say about an attack?"

"Early in the morning, there will be a major offensive against this area!" the German said fervently. "I told your captain, but he wouldn't believe me!"

"Why did you desert?"

"Because I hate the Army and the Nazis, and I couldn't take it anymore. My country is being destroyed."

Mahoney sat on his cot and puffed his cigarette, wondering if the German was telling the truth. He decided he couldn't do anything about it either way, so he stretched out on the cot, rested his head on his arm, and blew smoke rings toward the ceiling.

On the German side of the Siegfried Line, Field Marshall Walther Model stood with his aides in the darkness and watched the troops and tanks of the Fifth Panzer Army advance to their attack positions. Moveable ramps had been brought up from the rear and laid on the dragon's teeth of the Siegfried Line, so that the tanks could pass over. All roads leading to the front had been covered with straw to muffle the sound made by the tracks of tanks and personnel carriers. Ammunition for the opening artillery barrage was being carried forward by hand, to save gas and avoid the noise that trucks would make. Military police roamed the lines making certain there was no unnecessary movement. Strict radio silence was being observed.

Field Marshall Model stood with his hands in his greatcoat pockets and thought about Operation *Wacht am Rhein* as the tanks and men streamed past him. He knew that Hitler was gambling everything on this offense, and he was one of the officers who thought it could not succeed. He'd told Hitler that there weren't enough tanks, men, and supplies to carry the attack all the way to Antwerp, but Hitler had disagreed. All Model could do was follow orders. He was commander of Army Group B, which comprised the three panzer armies that would participate in the attack. Hitler had transferred all responsibility to his shoulders, and he'd done his usual, thorough job, but deep in his heart he thought the war was lost.

He heard footsteps approaching in the darkness. Turning, he saw Lieutenant General Hasso von Manteuffel, barely five feet, four inches tall, a former German pentathlon champion and commander of the Fifth Panzer Army in whose sector Model stood. Like Model, Manteuffel also doubted that the attack could push all the way to Antwerp and had argued for more modest objectives.

Manteuffel saluted Model. "Everything is going smoothly so far," he said, standing stiffly and looking up to the taller Model, who nodded.

"Yes," replied Model, who wore a monocle in his right eye. "Let's hope that the Amis don't get suspicious."

"We've received no reports of changes in their dispositions."

Model looked at his watch. It was two o'clock in the morning. "We have just a little more time to go. Let's hope they stay unsuspicious."

* * *

At Eighth Corps headquarters in Bastogne, Corporal Donald Riley of Abbotsford, Wisconsin, sat with headphones on in front of a radio set. He was sleepy and anxious because it was a few minutes after two o'clock in the morning, and his relief had not yet shown up. He rubbed his eyes and tried to focus on the copy of *Stars and Stripes* spread open on the space in front of the radio set.

A hand came to rest on his shoulder. Riley turned around and saw Pfc Arnold Scheuer of Columbus, Ohio, his relief.

"What're you sneakin' up on me for!" Riley exploded.

"I'm not sneaking up on you."

"About time you got here." Riley stood and handed Scheuer the headphones.

Scheuer put them on and sat at the bench. "Anything going on?" he asked.

Riley gathered up his *Stars and Stripes*. "The krauts are on radio silence."

"Did you report it?"

"Of course I reported it."

"I wonder why they're on radio silence."

Riley looked askance at him. "You know what we do when we go on radio silence, don't you?"

Scheuer shrugged. "We're usually getting ready to attack."

"Right."

Riley turned and walked away. Scheuer took out pencil and paper because he intended to write his girlfriend back home. Then he turned the knob and scanned the airwaves, listening to the frequencies that the Germans usually used for transmission. He heard nothing except faint whistles and static. He picked up his pencil and wrote the date on the upper right-hand corner of the blank piece of paper. If the Germans were on radio silence, that was the problem of G-2 (Intelligence). Let them worry about it.

But in G-2, the report of radio silence was filed with the other reports of unusual activity behind the German lines. The consensus was that either the Germans were on maneuvers in the area, or they were trying to fool the Americans into thinking that an attack was about to be launched.

FOUR

At five-thirty in the morning, a thunderstorm of German artillery shells suddenly rained down on the American lines between Monschau in the north and Echternach in the south. In Clervaux, a few dozen shells landed near the MP station, blowing cobblestones into the air and shattering buildings. Mahoney had been fast asleep, and the initial shock wave of the explosions threw him out of bed. He grabbed for his carbine, but there was no carbine in his tiny cell. He looked at his watch, but the MPs had taken it from him.

"They're coming!" screamed the German soldier down the hall. "They're coming!"

Mahoney felt like a rat in a trap. His ears rang with the sound of explosions, and the floor of the cell trembled beneath his feet. His cell had no window, so he couldn't see what was going on. He was far enough beneath the ground to be safe from the artillery, but what if the building above him collapsed? He might suffocate in his basement cell.

"HEY!" he bellowed, getting to his feet. "LET ME OUT OF HERE!" He pounded on his cot and rattled the bars of his cell. "LET ME OUT!"

The German soldier down the corridor continued to scream and other soldiers scattered throughout the cellblock hollered and banged around. The artillery barrage intensified, and it sounded like hell had broken loose in the town above. A squad of MPs came down to the cellblock to see what was going on.

"UNLOCK THESE CELLS!" Mahoney yelled.

"Shut up!" one of the MPs said.

"What's going on up there?"

"The krauts are sending us a little artillery, but it ain't nothin' to worry about. It should be over soon. You people down here had better calm the fuck down, if you know what's good for you."

Mahoney paced back and forth in his cell like a caged animal. The MPs left the cellblock and went back upstairs. The German artillery shells continued to fall like hail on the town of Clervaux.

Behind the artillery barrage, the tanks and men of the three panzer armies poured through the mountain passes toward the American positions in the Ardennes. The tanks were painted white, and the men wore white camouflage suits. There was a total of twenty-eight German divisions against six American divisions, and the German tanks and soldiers rolled easily over the American forward positions. The artillery barrage had destroyed most of the American communications network, so at first each isolated group thought that only it was under attack. The American units on the front lines fell back and coalesced, offering resistance wherever they could. They didn't know it yet, but they were being swept up in one of the biggest land battles in the history of the world.

The German artillery continued to shell American strongpoints after the assault was underway, and one of these strongpoints was the little town of Clervaux. Mahoney sat on his cot and looked at the dark ceiling as exploding shells caused a continuous roar in his ears. Although he had no idea of the scope of the German offensive, he knew that something serious was going on in the Clervaux sector at least.

He was hungry and wished he had a cigarette. He felt alone and vulnerable because usually in times of stress he was with his buddies in the Hammerhead Division. They worked together like a team and usually did okay, but here he was just an unarmed prisoner in a stockade.

A door opened down the corridor, and he heard a cacophony of footsteps. MPs appeared in the corridor, and one of them inserted a key into the lock on Mahoney's door.

"What's going on?" Mahoney asked.

"Get out of there," the MP said.

Mahoney stepped out of the cell into the corridor. He saw

other cells being opened and other imprisoned GIs spilling into the corridor and looking around, curious as he was. A dozen MPs were bustling around, along with a captain and two lieutenants. The floor shook from the impact of explosions, and small pieces of plaster fell from the ceiling.

Mahoney and the other prisoners were herded together in the middle of the corridor facing the MP captain.

"You can hear what's going on," the captain said. "The Germans have launched an all-out attack in this sector, and we need everybody we can get at the front. You men will be issued weapons and marched forward along with everybody else. If you give a good account of yourselves, it will be taken into consideration at your pending court martial proceedings."

The prisoners fell in and followed the MPs toward the door. Behind them, the German prisoner in his cell screamed in German, "I told you, but you wouldn't believe me!"

They climbed a flight of stairs and entered the main floor of the MP station. The sound of the barrage was much louder, and MPs walked around crouched over. Some huddled behind windows, peering out fearfully.

Mahoney and the other prisoners were told to wait in one corner of the room while the captain and other MPs conferred in another corner. Mahoney looked out a window and saw the gray light of dawn against the building across the street. He was standing next to an old beefy faced corporal who hadn't shaved for four or five days.

"Big fucking deal," the corporal muttered. "We'll go out and get killed, and it'll be taken into consideration at our court martials. Fuck that shit. I'd just as soon stay in the stockade."

"What're you in for?" Mahoney asked.

The corporal shrugged. "I was drunk and disorderly a few days ago, and they say I hit an MP, but I don't remember it." He leaned closer to Mahoney and whispered, "You wanna bug out?"

"No," Mahoney said.

The corporal made a face that indicated he thought Mahoney was a fool for not wanting to bug out, but Mahoney couldn't bring himself to run away from the enemy. Mahoney wasn't exactly an all-American boy, but he was no coward. He looked across the room to the MPs and spotted the swarthy one who'd hit him in the ribs with the billy club.

"Hey," Mahoney said to the corporal, "do you know the name of that MP over there with the face like a rat?"

"They all look like rats to me."

"The one third in from the left. He's a Pfc."

"That's Santucci. Watch out for him. He's a real prick of misery."

"What's your name?"

"Frazer."

"I'm Mahoney."

"What's a Hammerhead doing up here in the Eighth Corps?"

"It's a long story."

A first lieutenant came over to them and looked at them with obvious distaste. "We're going to the armorer now for weapons. Follow me, and keep your heads down. We're going to be watching you birds pretty closely, and anyone who tries to run away will be shot down. Any questions?"

Nobody said anything.

The first lieutenant continued, "We'll leave as soon as the steel helmets are brought up from downstairs. Are any of you in the combat arms?"

Mahoney, Frazer, and one other GI raised their hands.

"You three, step forward."

Mahoney and the others advanced toward the first lieutenant. He looked them over, apparently not satisfied with what he saw. "What were you with?" he asked the private on the left.

"Infantry."

"What about you?" the first lieutenant asked Frazer.

"I was a tanker," Frazer said.

The first lieutenant sidestepped in front of Mahoney and noticed the master sergeant stripes on his arm. "What about you?"

"Infantry," Mahoney said.

The lieutenant noticed Mahoney's Hammerhead patch. "What are you doing here?"

"TDY."

"Have you seen any combat?"

Mahoney nodded.

"I'm putting you in charge of these other men until further notice. What's your name?"

"Mahoney."

"I'm Lieutenant Baker."

The MPs came up from the cellar with crates filled with steel helmets and helmet liners that they'd taken from the various GIs who'd passed through their prison. The helmets were distributed, and Mahoney loosened the headband in his all the way before putting it on. The old familiar weight felt good on his head now that artillery shells were falling everywhere.

The lieutenant moved off and conferred with the captain. An artillery shell landed in the street outside, and everybody dropped to the floor, looking around fearfully. A second artillery shell landed on the roof of the MP station, and although that was two stories up, it sent plaster and timbers crashing down to the first floor.

The MPs and prisoners crowded against the walls or tried to crawl under desks. Mahoney spat dust and wished they'd get moving. The worst thing to do was to stay in one place while an artillery barrage was going on. He wished he was back in his old platoon where he gave the orders.

Plaster and wood stopped falling to the floor. The room was filled with billows of white dust. The MP captain scrambled to his feet and told Lieutenant Baker to get his men moving.

"Let's go!" said Lieutenant Baker to Mahoney and the other prisoners.

They ran out of the MP station to the cobblestone street which was filled with debris. Fires burned in some of the buildings, and civilians ran in all directions. Lieutenant Baker and his prisoners moved along swiftly, darting into doorways and falling onto their bellies in gutters whenever it sounded like a German shell or some screaming-meemies would land closeby. Gradually, they made their way through the town and Mahoney wondered how far away the Germans were and how soon it would take for reinforcements to arrive. He realized that Patton had been right to worry about the weakness of the Ghost Front.

Finally, at the eastern edge of the town, they encountered

clusters of soldiers and trucks parked in the streets. The soldiers huddled underneath the trucks, squeezed into alleys, or hid in cellars, their helmets and beady eyes visible through basement windows.

They came to a building that had a regimental flag hanging outside it. Lieutenant Baker told the men to wait for him and then went inside. Mahoney and the others sat on the sidewalk with their backs leaning against the building. For the first time, he became aware of the din of battle farther east. The Germans were heading this way—there was no doubt about it. If they wanted to strike deeper into Belgium, they'd have to come through Clervaux.

Mahoney looked around and counted the prisoners. One was missing already, and he realized that it was Frazer. The son of a bitch had flown the coop just like he said he would. It had been a foolish thing to do because if he got caught, they'd probably put him up against a wall and shoot him for desertion in the face of the enemy.

Lieutenant Baker came out of the building and told the men to follow him. He led them around the corner and into a building where rifles and ammunition were being issued in the basement. Mahoney was given a new carbine, still smelling of cosmoline. He was also issued a cartridge belt, bayonet, canteen, first aid packet, four bandoliers of ammunition, six hand grenades, and a field jacket with liner.

Armed to the teeth, Mahoney felt relieved. When all the prisoners were prepared for battle, Lieutenant Baker led them back to the building that had the regimental flag flying in front.

The streets in the area rapidly filled with soldiers. Some wore cooks' hats and others had the pale features of clerks who spent all their time indoors. They were scraping together every available man, which meant that the front was cracking.

Mahoney and the other prisoners entered an alley that already was crowded with GIs. Artillery shells whistled overhead and exploded on the roofs of buildings all around them. The air was thick with dust and gunpowder smoke, and some of the men coughed.

Mahoney bummed a cigarette from one of the soldiers and

then bummed a light. He took a few puffs and passed the cigarette to a young prisoner with blackheads and yellow crested pimples all over his face.

"What's your name?" Mahoney said.

"Riegle," the soldier replied between puffs.

"What'd you do?"

Riegle smiled, showing brown crooked teeth. "I shot an officer."

Riegle handed the cigarette to another prisoner who had a scar on his chin and tufts of black hair growing out of his nose.

"What'd you do?" Mahoney asked him.

"AWOL," the man replied.

Mahoney looked at the next man. "How about you?"

The man was tall and lanky with a rust mustache. "I tried to heist the 106th Division payroll," he said with a wink.

"What about you?" Mahoney asked the next soldier, whose eyes turned down at the corners and appeared angry at everybody and everything.

"They said I tried to rape some fucking nurse, but she was lying."

"Sure she was," Mahoney replied. He looked at the last soldier. "How about you?"

The last soldier had blond hair and a pink innocent baby face. "I was with him," he pointed to the one with the rust mustache, "on the payroll heist."

Mahoney groaned. "What a bunch of winners you guys are."

"What'd you do, Sarge?" asked baby face.

"I cut up some scumbag in a bar."

"Don't sound like you're any better than us."

The butt of the cigarette came back to Mahoney, and he took the last puff, realizing that baby face had said the truth. Mahoney had been in one of the crack outfits in the Army, but now he was just another criminal in uniform. He wondered if the sergeant he'd cut up had died.

On the street, soldiers climbed into the cabs of trucks and started up the engines. Officers blew whistles and hollered that everyone should load onto the trucks.

"Let's go," Mahoney said to his crew of prisoners.

They moved quickly into the street and climbed into the

back of a deuce and a half truck that had no canvas cover. The temperature was below freezing, and Mahoney knew it was going to be a very cold trip. They sat and waited as shells fell around them, and one landed in the street behind them, knocking a truck onto its side and throwing soldiers into the air.

"I'm getting out of here!" shouted red mustache.

He jumped up, but Mahoney rose with him and grabbed him by the throat. "You're not going anywhere," Mahoney told him, their noses almost touching.

Red mustache looked at Mahoney and stopped struggling. Mahoney threw him back into his seat.

"You fucking jailbirds are going to be soldiers from now on," Mahoney said, "or else you'll have to deal with me."

The rapist snickered. "Hey Sarge, if you keep talking like that, you'd better not turn your back on anybody!"

Mahoney spun around, grabbed him by his collar, and yanked him to his feet. "What'd you say!" Mahoney bellowed in his face.

The rapist struggled to get loose, but Mahoney had a strong arm and held him tighter. "I asked you a question, lover boy!"

The rapist trembled with fear, and his eyes darted about wildly. "I didn't say nothin', Sarge."

"Oh yes you did," Mahoney told him. "You said you were going to shoot me in the back. Well you'd better not miss because if you do, I'll break you in half."

The rapist nodded his head, and Mahoney pushed him down into his seat. Mahoney stayed erect and looked each of his men in the eye to make sure they all knew he was serious. The cooks and bakers in the truck glanced at each other, wishing they were on a truck with different people. Engines growled, and Mahoney turned to see the lead trucks pulling out. He sat in his seat as the truck lurched forward over the cobblestones.

Next stop—the front, Mahoney thought.

The convoy rolled slowly out of town. Armored personnel carriers with twin .50 caliber machine guns joined in from side streets along with four tank destroyers.

The convoy gathered speed and roared down the road leading east. The soldiers tried to get low and hide their faces and hands from the bitter cold. Artillery shells fell on the road, and Mahoney figured the Germans must have had it zeroed in for days. Several times the convoy had to drive on the shoulder to get around shell craters. Mahoney felt strange to be among soldiers he didn't know. He couldn't rely on these men, and a few of them might in fact try to shoot him in the back. The cooks and bakers weren't real soldiers and probably wouldn't last long in a hot fight. If his jailbirds didn't try to kill him, they'd probably go AWOL at the first opportunity.

The truck rocked and bounced over the road. Mahoney cupped his hands over his ears because they stung with the cold, and he thought they might get frostbitten. Next time he was tapped for TDY someplace, he'd tell them to shove it. If he got out of the mess he was in, he'd never leave old Charlie Company again.

"GET DOWN!" somebody shouted.

The GIs tried to hug the steel floor of the truck as a squadron of German fighter planes dived down from the clouds at them, their machine guns chattering and lightning flashing on their wings. The gunners atop the personnel carriers swung their .50s around and opened fire, but the German planes kept coming, their bullets ripping into the convoy.

Mahoney heard bullets hitting the truck and gritted his teeth as the planes passed by. Somebody screamed, and one of the cooks writhed and spurted blood.

Mahoney raised his head. "Is there a medic on this fucking truck?"

Nobody answered. Mahoney clawed men out of the way and saw the cook going into convulsions on the floor of the truck, blood pouring from his chest and back. The German bullet had gone clear through him, and Mahoney could see that nothing could be done. It'd only be a matter of time before the cook stopped moving and died.

Mahoney looked up and saw the German planes turning around in a wide circle beneath the cloud layer. He realized they were going to make another pass.

"Fire back at those planes!" he ordered. "It's the only way to spoil their aim and keep them off us!"

"Are you fucking crazy?" said Riegle, quivering with fear on the floor of the truck.

Mahoney grabbed him by the back of the neck and squeezed hard. "Never mind what I am—just do what I say!"

"Lemme go!"

Mahoney tightened his grip, then let him loose. Mahoney unslung his carbine, rammed a clip into the chamber, and then slammed a round into it. The men loaded their rifles and carbines and pointed them toward the sky. The German fighter planes had reformed and were coming in low and steady for their second strafing run. Mahoney rested his elbow on the roof of the cab, aimed at the lead plane, and opened fire. The lead plane roared closer, and Mahoney followed it in his sights, swinging around and shooting at its belly and tail as it passed by. Then, he aimed at the next plane and pulled the trigger of his carbine, making it buck and stutter in his hands. The other men in the truck fired their weapons, the excitement of the action sweeping them away. German bullets whizzed down at the trucks, and another man in Mahoney's group was torn apart by one of the big bullets. The last plane in the formation stitched bullets along the length of the truck and cut down two more men, but as it passed by, a trail of smoke could be seen pouring from the forward part of its belly.

Mahoney jumped into the air. "We got him!" he yelled.

"Yeah—we got him!" shouted baby face, waving his M-1 rifle in the air.

"He's going down!" said red mustache.

The German plane banked to the side and dipped its port wing, as the machine gunners on the personnel carriers directed deadly streams of machine gun bullets at it. Mahoney watched the tracers from the personnel carriers zip through the air, and black smoke belched out of the plane as it rolled onto its side and fell. It exploded on contact with the earth, and Mahoney cheered along with the men on his truck.

The other planes continued flying west to Clervaux, which Mahoney figured was in for a terrible pounding. Meanwhile, the convoy continued to make its way toward the fighting. Explosions ahead could be heard more clearly, and the men on Mahoney's truck kept their heads low to stay out of the cold windstream. The dead cook's blood was congealing around his wounds, but the men were growing used to it.

Twenty minutes later the convoy slowed down. Mahoney raised his head and saw soldiers ahead on both sides of the road. They were digging in behind rock and sandbag barricades on the flat ground beside the road or taking positions on the steep hills bordering the flat ground. Mahoney could see that the position would be a strong one because German tanks could advance only two or three abreast in the space between the hills. They wouldn't be able to mass their strength very well, and the meager American forces should be able to hold them off until help arrived.

The trucks stopped and officers ordered the men to unload. Mahoney and the others jumped down and stood around shivering, stamping their feet to get some warm blood moving into them. The trucks turned around and headed back to Clervaux.

A captain wearing the patch of the veteran Twenty-eighth Division approached and said, "Come with me!"

Mahoney and the others followed him to the right side of the line and up the hill to a cave thirty yards above the level of the road. He told some of the men to take positions in the cave, then deployed the rest up the side of the mountain and along the first ridge.

Mahoney and his jailbirds wound up on the ridge. The officer told them he'd send up some bazookas and machine guns as soon as they arrived. He put Mahoney in charge and descended the hill.

Mahoney stood on the ridge and looked in the direction of the German lines. He couldn't see very far because it was a hazy, cloudy morning, but he could hear artillery explosions and small arms fire. He wished he had binoculars and some cigarettes.

"Anybody got the time?" he asked.

"It's 0700 hours," said somebody.

The ridge was covered with ice and swept by cold winds carrying bits of snow. Mahoney lay on his stomach and felt the winter bite into his knees. Figures appeared on the road leading from the front, and as they drew closer, Mahoney could see that they were bedraggled American soldiers retreating. They stumbled along the road, carrying rifles, mortar tubes, and machine guns. American tanks came into view behind them, kicking up snow as they sped to safety. The soldiers on the road got out of the way so the tanks could pass. The tanks rolled past the fortifications and continued toward Clervaux.

"Hey—why don't they stop!" said the rapist.

Red mustache chortled. "Who's gonna stop them—you?"

The retreating soldiers were held up by officers and ordered into positions on the barricades. Then engineers with big pancake mines were sent out, dropping them onto the road and narrow strips of snow covered field alongside the road. The Germans would be able to see the mines easily silhouetted against the snow, but they'd have to stop anyway to dispose of them. That would slow them down and make them easy targets.

Everybody waited for the Germans to arrive. It would be the first time in combat for many of the green soldiers, and the veterans still hadn't gotten over the horror of the Hurtgen Forest. Mahoney began to think that the Germans would break through without much trouble if they really came in force.

Lieutenant Baker climbed to the ridge and spotted Mahoney. He walked toward him and blew his whistle, making a circle above his head with his forefinger, indicating that everyone should assemble around him. The soldiers arose from the icy rocks and walked stiffly toward him.

"All right men," Lieutenant Baker said grimly, "we're in a helluva fix here, and there are no two ways about it. The krauts are coming, and we've got to hold them off until reinforcements get here. If they break through, they're liable to go all the way to Liederveld where we've got our big gas dumps. If the krauts ever get their hands on that gas, we might as well kiss this part of the world goodbye. We can't let them get through—that's all there is to it. Reinforcements are on the way as I said. We can hold them if we dig in and fight hard. Any questions?"

Mahoney raised his hand. "When will the replacements get here?"

"I can't say for sure," Lieutenant Baker replied, his cheeks cherry red from the bitter winds. "Oh yes, there's something else you'd better know about: We've received reports that there are krauts behind our lines wearing American uniforms and talking English as well as you or me. This means we've all got to be suspicious of strangers and not take anything for granted. Anything else?"

"How about some chow?" Mahoney asked.

"We've got C rations down on the road. Send two of your men with me to pick them up."

Mahoney sent baby face and AWOL with the lieutenant, then turned to the front again. The engineers had finished work, and Mahoney could see the mines lying on the road and snow. They covered an area nearly a hundred yards deep, and he figured the Germans ought to be stopped for a while by them. The tank destroyers were in position, and bazooka teams ringed the valley. It looked like a decent defense, but Mahoney didn't think it would stop a lot of tanks for long. The best way to fight tanks was with other tanks, and all the American tanks had hightailed it to the rear.

Baby face and AWOL returned, each with two crates of C rations. Mahoney opened the crates with his bayonet and passed out the smaller boxes inside. The men tore them open for the canned food and cigarettes. Mahoney took a box for himself and was gratified to find a package of Lucky Strikes, his favorite brand, inside. He opened a can of beans with the tiny can opener provided and dug in with his fingers because they hadn't been issued mess gear. He hurried with his meal so he could have a cigarette.

"Here they come!" somebody yelled.

Mahoney looked toward the front but couldn't see anything. Glancing around, he saw officers down at the roadblock with binoculars, and he figured they could see what he couldn't. The Germans were coming. The shit was about to hit the fan again.

"All right everybody—get down!" he said.

The soldiers on the ridge got onto their bellies and squinted at the gray and white haze in front of them. It was a gloomy day with thick oily clouds covering the sky. Mahoney burped and lit a cigarette. He took out his bayonet and chipped some ice from the rock he was lying on, placing the ice in his mouth to slake his thirst.

Then he heard the hum of engines. He looked down the road and saw a dark mass in the distance. Glancing up to the sky, he saw tiny black dots.

"ENEMY PLANES!" somebody yelled.

"Where's our planes?" somebody else asked.

"If their planes can fly, why can't ours?" another soldier replied.

The German planes were in two squadrons, and they peeled off for their strafing and bombing run. Their engines became louder and sent chills up Mahoney's back. Didn't somebody say that bazookas and machine guns would be sent to the ridge? Where in the fuck were they?

The Germans bombed the minefield, hoping to blast a path for the tanks speeding down the road. They strafed the American positions from side to side, and Mahoney held his helmet onto his head with both hands, praying that somehow he wouldn't get hit. Violent explosions shook the ground and blew soldiers into the air. Machine gun bullets zipped into the bodies of GIs lying on their stomachs. American machine gunners fired back, and Mahoney looked up to see one of the planes in a tailspin, black smoke trailing from its fuselage. The German tank column approached on the road. The tanks opened fire, and Mahoney found himself in a holocaust of explosions, flying shrapnel, smoke, and screams. He realized that the position on the ridge was too vulnerable, and if he wanted to live a little longer, he'd have to go someplace else.

"LET'S GET OUT OF HERE!" he yelled, jumping to his feet.

He ran across the ridge and down the incline as the world exploded all around him. In the corner of his eye, he saw a bunch of soldiers at the barricades on the road blown into the air. He needed shelter fast. He remembered passing some caves on the way up to the ridge and headed for the nearest one. A piece of flying shrapnel ripped into the outer thigh muscle of his leg, and he fell, rolling over and tumbling down the hill, hugging his carbine close to him because that was one thing he didn't dare to lose.

He landed, scraped and bruised, at the bottom of the hill. Blood oozed from the wound in his thigh. Looking up, he saw six German tanks forming a long skirmish line, evidently preparing to attack. They fired their cannons, and the planes continued to drop bombs and to strafe.

"IN HERE!" somebody yelled.

Mahoney turned around and saw the opening to a cave.

Rocks had been piled in front of it, and he could see American helmets and the barrel of an anti-tank gun above the rocks. Mahoney got to his feet, ran eight steps, jumped, and soared over the rocks, landing inside the cave. He rolled over and looked around.

Eight sorrowful-looking GIs were there. The highest rank was a sergeant first class, which meant Mahoney suddenly had become the top man in the position. His leg felt as if a burning coal was pressed against it. Getting to his knees, he pulled out his bayonet and cut away the cloth around the wound. Blood wasn't spurting out, which meant that no artery was cut, and the bone evidently hadn't been broken because he'd been able to run on it. It was a nasty flesh wound, but he'd had them before and knew they weren't fatal. Opening his first aid pack, he took out the dressing and tore off the wrapper.

"Don't look too bad," said a corporal nearby.

Mahoney grunted as he tied on the dressing. Hopefully, it would hold the blood and cause it to coagulate. The cave echoed with the sound of explosions outside, and the tanks roared their engines.

"What's wrong with that anti-tank gun!" Mahoney said.

The soldiers in the cave looked at each other in embarrassment.

"Well," said the SFC, "we're not sure exactly of how to fire the goddamn thing. None of us here has ever seen one of these things close up before. You see, we're all from the Fourth Division band."

Mahoney groaned. He was stuck with a bunch of trumpet players and drummer boys. "Is there any ammo for it in here?"

"In those boxes over there," said a Pfc. "Don't you think that maybe we should surrender?"

"What for?" Mahoney asked. "We haven't even fired the goddamn thing yet. Bring that crate of ammo over here."

Mahoney got behind the gun and looked through the sights. He gulped as he saw the German tanks moving into the mine field. They weren't even going to take the time to send men to clear the mines away. They just were charging ahead, figuring they had so many tanks they could afford to lose a few.

The musicians brought the crate over and laid it at Mahoney's feet. They'd already removed the cover, and Mahoney plucked out one of the shells. He unlatched the backplate of the gun, loaded it, and took aim. He brought the crosshairs to rest on one of the lead tanks, but the tank was rocked by an explosion from a mine before Mahoney could pull the trigger. A tread blew into the air and the tank was unable to move forward, but its firing systems were undamaged, and its cannon fired a shell at the barricade.

Something told Mahoney to look behind him. Sure enough, one of the musicians was behind the anti-tank gun, sitting on his haunches and looking mournful.

"Get away from there!" Mahoney said.

"Whatsa matter?" the musician asked.

"I said, get the fuck away from there!"

The musician crawled away, and Mahoney took aim at the damaged tank again. He pulled the trigger, and the anti-tank gun went light on its tripod for a second as the shell flew out, and the backblast hit rocks and pebbles like a hurricane. If that musician had stayed behind the anti-tank gun, the backblast would have blown him apart.

The shell hit the tank in a ferocious thunderclap, and the tank disappeared in a cloud of black smoke.

"Hey—you got it!" said the SFC.

Mahoney loaded another shell into the gun, took aim, and fired. His shot was wide, and the shell exploded into the snow. Then the cave was rocked by a German artillery shell landing near the entrance. The interior of the cave echoed the sound, and Mahoney thought his eardrums would burst from the horrible noise. He'd known that once he fired the anti-tank gun, the Germans would see it and fire back. Another German shell landed near the mouth of the cave, and again Mahoney had to cover his ears with his hands. When the smoke cleared, he looked out of the cave and saw the tanks moving steadily forward to breach the defensive line at the road. Mahoney wondered why the American tank destroyers weren't doing anything. They should have been able to pick off the German tanks by now, but it appeared that the only tanks out of action had been damaged by mines and anti-tank or bazooka fire.

The tank drivers gunned their engines and charged through the minefield. Two more were stopped, but the rest kept going and passed out of Mahoney's line of vision. He didn't want to stick his head out of the cave to see what was going on because he thought he'd lose it. However, it didn't take much imagination to figure it out. The tanks had broken through the minefield and were rolling toward the sandbag positions on the road. He heard them crash through the sandbags, and their next stop would be Clervaux.

A few of the disabled German tanks still had operational cannons and machine guns. Mahoney loaded up the anti-tank gun again, took aim at one of them, and fired. The tank blew apart, chunks of metal and lengths of men's torsos flying into the air.

The other anti-tank gun crews fired at the remaining German tanks, which were all soon knocked out. The battlefield became silent, except for a few stray rifle shots and the chatter of machine guns. Mahoney squinted through the smoke and tried to see if any German infantry was coming, but he couldn't spot any. It had been a classic blitzkrieg tank attack, supported by planes and intended to make a quick deep penetration.

"Let's go," Mahoney said to the musicians in the cave.

"Go where?" asked a corporal.

"To make sure there aren't any live Germans in those tanks."

Mahoney led the musicians out of the cave and looked toward the roadblock. The carefully laid out positions had been devastated by the tank attack. Huge shell craters were everywhere, littered with bodies. The tank destroyers were gone, and Mahoney wondered if they'd been told to pull back or had retreated on their own.

The other survivors approached the smoking German tanks. Like Mahoney, they wanted to make sure there were no live tankers to take potshots at them while they were figuring what to do next.

Mahoney held his carbine ready as he limped toward the nearest tank. Huge fissures were in the turret and body of the vehicle. Mahoney stopped and looked inside. He saw blood already freezing and mangled, disjointed bodies.

"This one's okay," he told his men.

They walked to the next tank, but other soldiers were

already there. A few shots rang out—evidently some Germans weren't completely dead. Mahoney looked east down the road. No German soldiers were in sight, but more would arrive before long. He thought it would be a good idea to get away from that roadblock.

He and the other soldiers who'd gone to mop up the tankers returned to the ruined barricades. He saw a few trucks and jeeps that appeared undamaged and a lot of dead Americans. The frosty air smelled like the inside of a meat cooler in a butcher shop. Mahoney saw an American soldier who'd been shot neatly through the head. Something gleamed on the soldier's wrist, and Mahoney kneeled to see if the watch was still working.

"Whataya doing?" asked a passing soldier.

"What does it look like I'm doing?" Mahoney replied, unstrapping the watch.

"You're stealing from the dead!"

Mahoney ignored the soldier because his leg hurt and he didn't feel like wasting energy in a stupid argument. The watch was a new Bulova with a sweep second hand and a gold case. On the back was inscribed, *To Dennis from Margaret*. Mahoney strapped the watch to his wrist. It was nine-thirty in the morning. Mahoney opened the soldier's field jacket and took half a pack of cigarettes.

Mahoney spotted a group of men crowded around an officer and decided to go over and find out if the officer had any bright ideas. He headed in that direction, stepping over bodies and portions of bodies. Then he noticed something gleaming on the shoulder of a dead soldier. It was a first lieutenant's silver bar, and Mahoney wondered if it was Lieutenant Baker.

Mahoney kicked him onto his back. It was Lieutenant Baker. A piece of shrapnel had torn through his chest and stomach, and his steaming guts spilled out of him.

Mahoney noticed binoculars lying near Lieutenant Baker's face. Picking up the binoculars, he wiped the snow from the lenses and saw that they weren't cracked. He looked through the binoculars; they worked perfectly. Hanging them from his neck, he spied a gold watch on Lieutenant Baker's wrist. It's always good to have two watches in case one of them gets broke, he thought. He took the watch, a Longines, from the lieutenant's wrist and strapped it to his own next to the Bulova.

Mahoney lit one of his Luckies and walked toward the group of soldiers crowding around the officer. As Mahoney drew closer, he could see that the officer was the captain who wore the patch of the Twenty-eighth Division. He had a map spread on the hood of a jeep and was tracing his finger over the road.

Mahoney bulled his way through the soldiers. "If you're looking for a different road back to Clervaux," he said to the captain, "I know of one that's pretty good."

The captain had broad shoulders and a barrel chest. He was freshly shaved and exuded purposeful energy. "Show me on the map."

Mahoney bent over the map and placed his finger on a road he'd used on a recent reconnaissance trip. "This road isn't as good as the one we're on, but it's nearly as good. If we get rolling right now, maybe we can beat those krauts back to Clervaux."

"It's worth a try," the captain said. He raised his arm in the air and waved toward the trucks. "LOAD IT UP! WE'RE MOVING OUT!"

Mahoney headed toward the trucks, but the captain stopped him. "What's your name?"

"Mahoney."

"I'm Captain Carlson. Are you Infantry?"

"Yes, sir."

"I thought so. You'll ride in this jeep with me."

"Yes, sir."

Mahoney climbed into the jeep and sat in the back. He turned up his collar and turtled his head inside because he knew it was going to be a cold son of a bitch on the way back. He lit another cigarette.

A Pfc got behind the wheel of the jeep and Captain Carlson sat beside him on the passenger seat. "You all right back there, Sergeant?" he asked Mahoney.

"Yes, sir."

Captain Carlson tapped the Pfc on the shoulder. "Move it out."

The Pfc shifted into gear and gave it the gas. The jeep's

rear wheels spun on the ice. The Pfc turned the jeep around and accelerated past the trucks and other jeeps that were waiting to follow Captain Carlson. Mahoney looked at his two watches and hoped they'd beat those German tanks to Clervaux. Captain Carlson pumped his arm up and down in the signal for *double-time*, indicating that he wanted everyone to drive as fast as they could.

The few trucks and jeeps pulled together into a mini-convoy and drove away from the scattered bodies and crimson snow.

FIVE

In Bastogne, General Troy Middleton was trying to make sense out of the scattered reports that he'd received. Several indicated that a few individual units had been overrun or cut off by Germans, but Middleton couldn't tell how serious or widespread the German attack was, or where it was going. His communications network had been damaged, and he was out of contact with many of his commanders. Finally he decided to call his superior officer, Lieutenant General Courtney Hodges, at First Army Headquarters in Luxembourg City.

It took a while to get through, but finally General Hodges came on the phone. General Middleton explained that his line had been pierced by the Germans in four or five places and requested reinforcements from other corps in the First Army to beef up the Eighth Corps Ghost Front.

General Hodges, a tall and lean gray-mustached man of 58, listened quietly and calmly to General Middleton's report and requests. An unusually soft-spoken and gentlemanly officer, Hodges was equal in rank and responsibilities to General Patton but was almost unknown to the American people because he had no talent or interest in self-promotion. He never wore bizarre uniforms and never engaged in flamboyant behavior. Yet his First Army had covered more ground in France than Patton's Third Army, and he'd commanded more armor than Patton. Whereas Patton was a creature of inspiration, Hodges was a cool, methodical worker, and he was said to be unshakeable in battle.

Hodges thought for several moments after Middleton stopped talking, and then said, "I'd like to have a better picture of your situation there before I divert other units from the missions they're on right now. How soon do you think you'll be able to report back to me?"

"I don't know, sir. My communications net is a mess."

"Then get it repaired and report back to me. Be as accurate as you can because I wouldn't want to break off attacks that presently are underway if it's not necessary. Is that clear?"

"Yes, sir."

"Carry on."

General Middleton hung up the phone and scratched his head. He'd wanted to argue with Hodges because he had the feeling that a dangerous situation was developing in the Eighth Corps sector, but he had no proof, so he hadn't said anything. Somehow he had to get the facts, but how could he get facts if his telephone communications net was out of whack?

He made a call to his communications officer, Colonel Denton. "Denton," he said, "what's the communications picture now?"

"Getting worse," Denton replied.

"You'd better get it fixed fast," Middleton said angrily. "I've got to find out what's going on."

"Sir, lines are being destroyed faster than my men can fix them, but we're doing our best."

Middleton knew that radio communications were out of the question, due to the difficulty of transmitting in mountainous areas. "You've got to do better than your best," he told Denton.

"I'll get right to work on it sir."

General Middleton hung up the phone and was more troubled than ever. It was inconceivable that the Germans could mount a full-scale attack at this stage of the war, but what if they had?

Middleton shook his head. That was too horrible to contemplate.

Mahoney's nose was buried in his collar, and his helmet was low over his eyes, but he thought he saw figures on the road up ahead. Braving the frigid windstream, he took his hands out of his pockets and raised his binoculars to his eyes as the jeep bounced over the icy road. The magnification showed three soldiers running toward a jeep.

"There's something up ahead!" Mahoney shouted above the roar of the engine.

Captain Carlson looked through his binoculars and saw the three men driving away toward Clervaux. "Looks like some of our people," he said.

"Didn't somebody say there are Germans wearing GI uniforms behind our lines?" Mahoney asked.

"That's right too. We'd better see what they were up to. Hathaway, slow down. They might have tossed some mines onto the road.

Hathaway braked, and Captain Carlson stood up to get a better look at the road ahead. "I don't see anything," he said. "Keep going slowly."

Hathaway drove forward in low gear, and Captain Carlson raised his hand to signal the trucks behind him to slow down. The jeep eased into an intersection that had directional arrows on a post. Captain Carlson and Mahoney jumped out and looked around. They saw jeep tracks in the snow and some footprints around the signpost. Mahoney checked the arrows and realized that the one for Clervaux was pointed in the wrong direction.

"Hey," said Mahoney, "the bastards fucked with the signs!"

"How do you know?" asked Carlson.

Mahoney pointed down the road. "Because Clervaux is thataway."

"We'd better fix the signs," Carlson said.

"I think we'd better tear them down and take them with us," Mahoney replied. "Otherwise somebody's liable to come by and fuck them up again."

"You're right. Take 'em down, Mahoney."

Mahoney trudged into the snow and batted the signs down with the butt of his carbine. He picked up the signs, carried them to the jeep, and dumped them in the back seat. Then he got in. Hathaway drove off toward Clervaux again. The other trucks and jeeps followed. Mahoney looked at his watch. He figured that Clervaux was only about half an hour away.

Ahead on the road was a jeep with three German SS men disguised as American GIs. They were Lieutenant Rolf Gurtner, and Sergeants Franz Muller and Ernst Grieser. Each had been born in Germany but raised in America, and they spoke American English perfectly. Gurtner and Muller were from the German neighborhood known as Yorkville in New York City, and Grieser was from Milwaukee, which also had a large concentration of German-Americans. In the thirties, each of them had become inspired by the Nazi movement in their native land and returned to become a part of it.

Gurtner held a captured U.S. Army map low so that the wind wouldn't disturb it. "We're almost in Clervaux," he said. "There is a large garrison there, and we have to cut their communications."

The other two SS men nodded. That's what they'd been doing all morning, in addition to changing road signs and giving inaccurate directions to any Americans who were lost. One of their missions behind the lines was to kill high-ranking American officers, but they hadn't seen any yet. They hoped they might find a general to shoot in Clervaux.

"Can't you get any more speed out of this piece of junk?" Gurtner asked Muller, who was driving.

"This is as fast as it will go," Muller replied.

Gurtner muttered something about the inadequacies of American manufacturing as the town of Clervaux came into view on the horizon. A cloud of dark smoke hung over the city and fires were raging in some of its neighborhoods. As the jeep drew closer, the extent of the devastation could be perceived by the three German commandos. Many buildings had been leveled by the bombing, and other buildings consisted only of a wall or two. Nearly every building had suffered some damage, and from the distance it appeared as though all human life had ceased in the town.

The three German commandos entered Clervaux, looking in all directions for communication lines to cut and Americans commanders to kill.

Fifteen minutes later, the convoy led by Captain Carlson and Mahoney entered Clervaux and made its way around rubble and devastated vehicles to a headquarters building in the center of town.

"You men wait out here," Captain Carlson said, "while I go inside to find out what we have to do."

Mahoney got out of the jeep, and the other soldiers jumped down from the trucks. They entered the buildings nearby so that they wouldn't be out in the open when the Germans started shelling again. They knew that the German armored column would arrive in Clervaux before long, and when it did, another battle would ensue.

Mahoney found himself in a store whose shelves had been stripped of goods. The signs and posters on the walls indicated that it had been a grocery. He sat on the floor and leaned his back against the wall.

He thought that maybe he should go to the MP station and destroy the records of his arrest, but the more he thought about it, the more he realized that might be hazardous. If the MPs still were in the station, they might remember him and lock him up again, or at least put him under guard. If they weren't there, they probably had taken their records with them.

The image of Madeleine flashed into his mind. He saw her sitting in the candlelight of the café, so frail and vulnerable. He knew that she'd liked him; a man always can tell when a woman likes him, even though she argues with him and gives him a hard time. It was a shame a woman like that had to be a whore. He wondered if she still was at the café and if she was all right. Maybe she needed some help right now. He wanted to see her again.

He got up and walked to the shattered front door of the store.

"Where you going?" asked one of the soldiers.

"Out to take a piss."

On the sidewalk, Mahoney slung his carbine over his shoulder and headed in the direction of the café. It was on the other side of town, but the town wasn't very big, and he didn't think it would take long to get there. He passed broken telephone poles and shell craters in the middle of streets. A few other soldiers were moving about, and smoke curled from burning piles of debris. The air had the rotten stink of burning, wet, old wood. Occasionally, he saw a jeep and ducked into a doorway until it passed. He knew that if he was seen by an officer, he'd be told to go someplace else.

Finally he came to the café. The street, which had been so serene and magical last night, was now a junkyard like the rest of the city. An artillery shell had hit the top of the building that housed the café, but there seemed to be little damage on the lower floors. The front window has broken and boarded up on the inside. Mahoney turned the doorknob, but the door was locked. He banged on the door with the butt of his carbine and listened, but heard nothing inside. He banged again, but still no one came. He decided to shoot his way through the door. Raising his carbine, he pulled back the bolt and took aim.

Just then the door opened a crack, and standing there was the bartender who'd served him last night. The bartender saw the carbine pointed at him, jumped back, and looked terrified.

"What do you want?" he asked.

Mahoney stepped inside the café and closed the door behind him. He looked around and in the dimness could see only vacant tables and a blanket over the piano that had been played so raucously the night before.

"Where are the girls?" Mahoney asked.

"They've all gone."

"Madeleine too?"

"Yes."

Mahoney pinched his lips together. "Shit!"

The bartender peered into his face. "You're the one who killed another soldier with a broken bottle here last night, aren't you?"

"Did I really kill him?"

"That's what I heard."

Mahoney pulled out his pack of cigarettes and offered one to the bartender, who took it. Then Mahoney put one in his own mouth. "You got anything to drink in here?"

"What would you like?"

"Brandy."

"Have a seat."

Mahoney sat at a table near the bar and looked at the one near the wall where he'd sat with Madeleine last night. He wondered where she was right now. Probably blowing some other GI, but somehow that didn't bother Mahoney very much. It was her job and all that mattered was that she'd have something for him if ever they met again.

The bartender returned from the back room with a bottle and two glasses. He sat and poured brandy, then lifted one of the glasses into the air. "To victory," he said.

"Yeah," Mahoney replied, taking a swig. "How come you haven't left town with everybody else?"

The bartender raised his chin. "This is my café. I've worked for most of my life to establish it, and I'll never leave."

"German money is as good as American money, I guess."

"A person has to live. I prefer the Americans and the British because they're not as cruel to us as the Germans, but I'm going to stay here regardless. What's the point in running every time the town changes hands? If I did that, I'd be running back and forth all the time."

Mahoney drank some more brandy and puffed his cigarette. "Tell me about Madeleine."

"What do you want to know about her?"

"Where's she from?"

"From Brussels, I think," the bartender replied. "She's a nice girl—provided you don't cross her. She has a terrible temper just like you. Once she attacked one of the girls with a nail file and cut her face up."

Mahoney smiled. "That's my baby."

"You are in love with her?"

"I don't know. Maybe."

"I think she liked you. She was very upset when the MPs took you away. She told everybody that you'd fought the other soldier because he was bothering her, and I had the impression that she was very grateful." The bartender winked.

"She'll probably show you a good time if ever you see her again."

"Think she'll be back here?"

"I don't know. It's hard to say about these girls. They're all a bunch of gypsies."

"If she comes back," Mahoney said, "tell her that I came by asking for her."

"I'll tell her," the bartender replied. "I'm sure she'll be very glad to hear that."

An artillery shell exploded in another part of town, and Mahoney perked his ears up. The bartender looked at the ceiling. Another shell exploded in the distance, and then another.

"The Germans are coming," the bartender said.

Mahoney pulled his canteen out of its cover. "I think I'll fill this up before I leave."

He poured the brandy into his canteen, threw a ten-dollar bill on the table, and walked toward the door.

"Good luck," the bartender said.

"You too," Mahoney replied.

Mahoney stepped onto the sidewalk wondering whether to participate in the defense of Clervaux or to head south where the Third Army was. He stood in a doorway and puffed his cigarette as shells fell on Clervaux with greater intensity. He decided that if he had to fight, he'd rather fight with his buddies, but he could never make it back to Third Army on foot, and he didn't want to steal a vehicle that might be needed in the fight here. He also didn't want to hide in a cellar like a rat until the battle for Clervaux was over. If the Germans took the town, he'd be in more trouble with them than he was in right now.

The only thing to do was go to the front and be a soldier. He came out of the doorway and walked toward the east side of town, where the Germans most probably would attack. He'd seen maps of the area and knew that the Germans would have to go right through Clervaux if they wanted to advance deeper into Belgium, because the town was ringed by hills and mountains impassable to armor.

A three-quarter ton truck turned the corner behind him and sped up the street. When the driver saw Mahoney, he hit the brakes, and the truck screeched to a halt. The driver stuck his head out the window. "Hey buddy—you want a lift?"

Mahoney ran toward the back of the truck, and arms came down to pull him aboard. The truck started moving again, and Mahoney sat on the wooden bench on the left wall of the cargo space, looking at four big brawny GIs. They carried no weapons and hadn't shaved for days.

"Where are you guys coming from?" Mahoney asked as the small truck rocked from side to side.

One of the soldiers pointed in a northerly direction. "We're loggers," he said. "We were working in the woods when they came for us."

"Loggers?" Mahoney asked. "You guys know how to fire rifles?"

"Yeah," said one of the others, "but they don't have any rifles for us yet. If they can't come up with any, we always can use these."

The soldier opened a big wooden toolbox, and Mahoney saw hatchets and axes inside.

"I don't know how good they'll be against tanks," Mahoney said, "but I suppose they're better than nothing."

Mahoney looked out the rear of the truck, seeing bombs exploding among the buildings. Occasionally he saw a civilian scurrying down a street or a small group of GIs moving toward the front. Mahoney wondered why it had taken this long for the German armored column to reach Clervaux. He figured that GIs must have fought a few delaying actions along the way.

Finally, the truck stopped. The driver came out to the back and said, "I can't go any farther. Everybody out."

The loggers took axes and hatchets out of their toolbox and jumped down with Mahoney. In front of the truck were some GIs building a roadblock out of bricks and lengths of timber taken from ruined buildings nearby.

A young second lieutenant was supervising the construction of the roadblock. "Hey you men!" he shouted to Mahoney and the others. "Get over here and help out!"

Mahoney walked toward the lieutenant and saluted smartly. "I'm sorry sir, but I've been ordered to report with my men to Captain Carlson at the front," he lied.

"All right," said the lieutenant. "Move 'em out."

"Let's go, men," Mahoney said to the loggers.

Mahoney led the loggers through the streets and could see that a defense was being established in depth. If the German tanks broke through one roadblock, they'd soon encounter another. Soldiers worked everywhere building fortifications and obstacles for the battle that was looming. Meanwhile, German artillery shells continued to fall on the town, and Mahoney didn't think there'd be much of the town left when this battle was over.

Finally, he and the loggers came to the edge of the town, where the biggest barricades were being constructed. Antitank guns and bazooka crews were deployed behind the barricades and in the buildings nearby. Machine gun nests were everywhere, and rifle soldiers threw bricks and wood onto the fortifications, their exhalations making gray clouds in the cold air.

An old lieutenant colonel noticed Mahoney and the loggers. "What unit are you men with?" he asked.

"No unit, sir."

"Then you might as well get to work right here."

Mahoney aimed his thumb behind him at the loggers. "These men don't have any weapons."

"We're expecting some to arrive soon. Meanwhile, there's a lot to be done. Report to Captain Devine." The lieutenant colonel pointed to an officer supervising some work nearby.

Mahoney and the loggers walked toward Captain Devine, who wore a wool overcoat with the collar up. He turned as Mahoney approached, and Mahoney saluted him. Captain Devine appeared cheerful, as if he looked forward to the battle. Mahoney figured he was from West Point because West Point graduates often acted that way. Evidently it was supposed to be inspiring to the men.

Captain Devine told them to work on the fortifications. "The krauts will be here pretty soon," he said. "We'll want to give them a warm reception."

Mahoney and the loggers joined the work gang. In the bitter cold, they carried bricks and debris, and threw them onto the wall being built on the edge of town. Mahoney grumbled and scowled because NCOs usually didn't do coolie work like this. They just supervised it. But there was no time for that nonsense now. The Germans were coming, and they wanted Clervaux. Pausing to take a break, he drank some brandy from his canteen. As he was returning his canteen to its case, he heard a faint hum in the distance. He raised his binoculars and scanned the horizon. Tiny dots were spread across the sky.

"GERMAN PLANES!" Mahoney shouted, running for his carbine, which he'd leaned against a stack of other rifles.

The officers and NCOs with binoculars looked through them and saw what Mahoney had seen.

"TAKE COVER!" shouted the old lieutenant colonel. "MAN YOUR GUNS!"

Mahoney ran to the barricade and lay behind it as soldiers he'd never seen before flopped down on either side of him. The dots on the horizon became larger, and soon the silhouettes of the aircraft could be seen. The machine gun crews opened fire, their tracer bullets making long red lines on the gray clouds. An anti-aircraft battery to the rear began pumping shells into the sky, and the German planes roared forward in attack formation. Orange sparks appeared along their wings as they opened fire, and their bullets ripped into the ground in long straight lines.

Mahoney could hear the bullets whamming into the ground all around him. He pulled his elbows in to his sides in an effort to make himself smaller, and breathed through clenched teeth. Then the light bombers came, dropping their loads. The ground shook with deafening explosions, and groups of soldiers were blown into the air. A few of the soldiers who'd been clerks or other kinds of service personnel broke and ran to the rear, screaming in terror, but most of the men stayed where they were and prayed that somehow they'd survive.

Some of the men running away were struck in the back and nearly broken in two by the power of the big German machine gun bullets. Mahoney looked up and saw planes as thick as hornets in the sky. Where's our air force? he wondered. It looks like these bastards have caught us with our pants down.

"HERE COME THE TANKS!" somebody yelled.

Mahoney peered over the barricade and saw tanks all over the road and fields leading to town. They were charging at top speed, shooting their cannons as they came. A bazooka crew near Mahoney fired at the tanks, but the rocket fell far short.

Mahoney cupped his hands around his mouth. "Wait till they get closer!"

The bazooka crew fired again, and that round fell short too. Mahoney realized that the men firing the bazooka probably hadn't seen one since basic training back in the States and didn't know what its effective range was. He'd have to go over and take charge.

Mahoney cradled his carbine in his arms and crawled toward the bazooka crew. He heard an artillery shell whistling down on him and stopped cold, certain it was going to land on his head. He held his helmet tight and squinched his eyes as he prayed to the Lord for deliverance. The artillery shell smacked into the ground nearby and blew chunks of ice and frozen sod into the air. Some of the small pieces landed on Mahoney, and a chunk two feet wide crashed a few feet from his head.

Mahoney resumed crawling toward the bazooka crew. The soldiers had stopped firing and were trying to stuff themselves into nooks and crannies to protect themselves from the mounting shellbursts, although the tanks were coming into range now and this was the time to fire the bazooka.

Mahoney reached the bazooka and put it onto his shoulder while rising to one knee. "One of you guys load this fucking thing up for me!" he shouted.

The soldiers wouldn't move. They hugged their helmets to their heads and tried to hide. A bullet ricocheted off the top of the barricade, and they squirmed even more frantically. One of them wore an MP armband. Mahoney laid down the bazooka and pulled the man up by his arm. "Hey—I just gave you an order!"

Mahoney found himself looking into the horrified face of Santucci, the MP who'd worked him over with a billy club.

"You son of a bitch!" Mahoney screamed and punched him in the mouth with all his might.

Santucci went out like a light. Mahoney wanted to pick him up and belt him again, but a German bomb came whistling down, and Mahoney dropped to his belly. The bomb exploded, blowing a length of the barricade into the air. Mahoney grabbed one of the other soldiers who was trying to claw his way deeper into the frozen ground. Mahoney held the soldier by the front of his field jacket and spoke so forcefully he spit all over the soldier's face. "Load this fucking bazooka!"

"Yes, Sergeant," the soldier said, trembling with fear.

Mahoney placed the bazooka on his shoulder and aimed at one of the huge tanks advancing toward the barricade. The soldier behind him tapped Mahoney's helmet, and Mahoney pulled the trigger. The rocket flew and landed directly on the tank's turret. It exploded, and the tank became wreathed in smoke, but seconds later the smoke dissipated, and there wasn't a scratch on the tank.

"Holy shit," Mahoney muttered, as the soldier loaded up the bazooka tube again. Mahoney took a good look at the tank and saw that it was bigger than any German tank he'd ever seen before. It had so much armor on its front that a bazooka shell did no damage. The only thing to do was to aim lower at the treads or let the tanks pass by and hit them in the rear where their armor was thinner and their ammunition racks were located. The soldier hit Mahoney's helmet again, and Mahoney fired at the tank's treads. He scored a direct hit, and the treads blasted apart, stopping the tank cold and causing it to tip toward its damaged side.

Now the tank was a stationary fortress, and its turret swung around as its commander looked for a target.

"Uh-oh," Mahoney said, wondering which way to run.

Just then, the tank was hit by an anti-tank shell, and once again it disappeared in an explosion and cloud of smoke. This time, when the smoke cleared, the tank was a pile of hot smoking scrap iron. The shell had pierced the tank's armor!

Near Mahoney, the crew of the anti-tank gun cheered.

"Load me up again," Mahoney told the soldier behind him.

The soldier pushed another rocket into the tube and tied the rocket's wires to the terminal posts. Mahoney aimed at the treads of another tank and pulled the trigger of the bazooka. The rocket flew forth slowly enough so that Mahoney could watch it, and it missed the treads of a tank by two yards.

"Load me up again!"

Machine gun fire raked the section of the barricade in front of Mahoney. Mahoney ducked instinctively, but the soldier behind him didn't move quickly enough, and he received a burst in his chest, breaking apart his ribs and shattering his lungs. He fell backwards and was dead before he hit the ground.

Mahoney lay on the ground until the machine gun fire moved to another part of the barricade. Then he raised himself and looked at the German tanks. They were closer, and he could see the black crosses distinctly on the turrets. Glancing around, his eyes fell on Santucci, the MP.

"You—load me up!" Mahoney said.

Santucci shook his head, and a trickle of blood ran from his nose where Mahoney had slugged him before. "I don't take orders from stockade rats!"

"Oh no?"

Mahoney punched him again, and Santucci collapsed.

"I'll load you up, Sergeant," said a youthful voice.

Mahoney turned and saw a kid with freckles on his nose. He looked sixteen years old and probably had lied about his age when he'd enlisted.

"Do it," Mahoney said.

Mahoney placed the bazooka on his shoulder. Men screamed farther down the line, and Mahoney saw a big fat German tank rolling over the barricade. The freckle-faced soldier tapped Mahoney's helmet, and Mahoney swung the bazooka around, aiming it at the rear of the tank. He licked his lips and pulled the trigger, watching the rocket speed through the air toward the tank. It slammed into the tank's rear deck and burst apart in a violent explosion. When the smoke cleared, the tank was stopped and smoke poured out of the black hole.

"Hey Sarge—we got him!"

Machine gun bullets whistled past their ears and both of them dived toward the ice and snow on the ground. Mahoney saw in the corner of his eye another tank breaching the barricade, firing its cannon at a building where a GI machine gun nest had been set up. Hearing the roar of an engine to his left, he looked and saw that tank rumbling over the barricade as soldiers ran in all directions to get out of its way.

Mahoney wanted to raise his head and try to knock out one of the tanks with his bazooka, but the barricade in front of him was being peppered with machine gun fire. Mahoney looked at the tank and cursed it when suddenly it exploded in an orange burst. For a split second, Mahoney thought his curse had destroyed the tank, but then common sense overtook him, and he realized that one of the anti-tank guns must have hit it.

The machine gun fire moved away from his barricade. Mahoney got to one knee again, feeling pain from the wound in his leg that he'd sustained earlier in the day. He looked down and saw blood seeping into the bandage. His movements and scraping against the ground must have opened the wound. He swore as the freckle-faced soldier loaded up the bazooka. Mahoney aimed it at the other tank that had broken through, but from out of nowhere, a GI ran at the tank with a hand grenade, stuffed the grenade into the treads of the tank, and sped off. The soldier dived to the ground, and the grenade exploded, ripping apart the tank's tread. The tank stopped, and its turret turned around as the tank commander looked for the soldier who'd done the damage. Mahoney wondered how the German tankers felt, knowing they were stationary targets. But they weren't stationary targets for long. An anti-tank shell hit them, WHAM, and the tank and crew were out of the war for good.

Mahoney turned to the front again and went pale at the sight of a German tank only twenty yards away, heading straight for him.

"LOAD ME UP!" Mahoney screamed.

The freckled-faced soldier tried to keep his trembling hands under control as he inserted the rocket into the tube and tied up the wires. Mahoney got as low as he could, aimed at the underbelly of the tank, and fired the rocket. It shot forward and hit directly where Mahoney had aimed it, exploding and blowing the tank's turret into the air.

Another tank was beside the tank Mahoney had hit, and its machine gun swung to the side as lightning shot out of its barrel.

"Get down!"

Mahoney dropped as bullets whizzed over his head. Looking behind him, he saw the kid hugging the ground too.

"I'm still here, Sarge," he said.

Several tanks breached the barricade and turned to the side to fire at the men behind it because the tankers knew by now that they didn't dare bypass live, armed GIs. The anti-tank emplacements in the buildings fired broadside at the tanks, knocking one after the other out of action, but the undamaged tanks rolled over GIs and fired their machine guns across the barricades.

Mahoney knew that the barricade was no longer a viable fortification, and more tanks breached the barricade because the GI's were too busy dodging bullets to shoot their bazookas at the tanks. Mahoney was afraid to run because he'd be an easy target for the tank's machine gunners, but if he stayed where he was, a tank would roll over him and grind him into the ground.

The kid tapped his helmet; through the intense fire he'd managed to load Mahoney up again. Mahoney aimed straight up at the belly of the tank bearing down on him and turned the rocket loose. It hit the tank low and on target, and the tank bounced two feet in the air, smoke and fire blasting through cracks in its hull.

"FALL BACK!" somebody shouted. "RETREAT!"

Mahoney turned to the kid behind him. "Let's go!"

The kid looked like he was going to cry. "We'll never make it!"

"We won't make it here either!"

Mahoney sprang to his feet and ran like a racehorse despite the pain in his leg. He zigzagged and dodged as bullets flew over his head and kicked up ice near his feet. Glancing to his left and right, he saw other soldiers dashing back to the next barricade, which was on the main boulevard of the town and extended between the buildings on both sides of the street. Blood dripped down his leg, but he summoned up his deepest reserves of energy and galloped over the final yards of ground to the barricade, vaulting over it, catching one toe on a piece of debris at the top, and falling face first behind it. He managed to get his hands up before he hit the ground, saving his nose from being mashed into his face.

Rolling over, his skin scraped from the palms of his hands, he got to his knees and tried not to think of the pain in his leg and the blood freezing on the bandage and his pantleg. He looked back to the German tanks and saw one of them burst into flame. The boulevard was littered with bodies of dead GIs, and Mahoney wondered what had happened to the kid. He glanced behind the barricade at red-faced GIs struggling for breath and realized with chagrin that the kid evidently hadn't made it.

Mahoney looked to the front again and saw a figure writhing on the road beside a crate of bazooka rockets. Mahoney raised his binoculars and could see the kid clawing the air, blood trickling from the corner of his mouth. Mahoney wanted to get him, but knew it would be suicide. The tanks were coming, and he wouldn't have a chance.

An anti-tank gun knocked out a tank that had been heading straight for the kid. Mahoney wished he had those rockets for the bazooka, but he'd never be able to get them. Or could he? The tanks appeared to be regrouping into something that resembled a flying wedge, and Mahoney thought he might be able to dash out there and get back if he moved quickly. Then, before his eyes, an anti-tank gun scored a direct hit on another tank behind the kid. Mahoney could see that those two knocked-out German tanks could provide a screen for him, because no other tanks could pass through them.

It's now or never, he thought. Laying the bazooka on the ground and leaning the carbine against the barricade, he uttered a silent prayer and leapt over the barricade. He swung his fists back and forth and ran as quickly as he could, not bothering to make zigzag lines and a low silhouette. He saw tanks moving and regrouping in the middle of the street, but to his front the kid was reaching out to him and next to the kid was the crate of bazooka rockets. Mahoney tried to stop suddenly when he neared the kid, tripped over his own feet, and pitched forward onto his face. Scrambling to his feet again, he picked up the kid and threw him over his shoulders. Then he bent his knees, tucked the crate of rockets under one arm, and headed back to the barricade.

His leg ached more than ever, and he thought it was going to give way beneath him as he raised his knees high and sped to safety. On his shoulders the kid groaned and dripped blood onto Mahoney's field jacket. Mahoney sucked wind and thought he didn't have the strength to go on. The kid and the crate of rockets were too much for him. But he kept running anyway and noticed a curious thing. No one was shooting at him. Either the Germans were too busy with whatever they were doing and didn't notice him, or they were going to let him make it. He'd never know which, but he reached the barricade anyway, dumped the kid over it, threw over the crate of rockets, and then collapsed over the top of it to safety.

"Medic!" he yelled as he hit the ground.

The old lieutenant colonel ran in a crouch behind the barricade toward Mahoney. "I saw that!" he said. "I'm putting you in for the DSC!"

The kid was gasping, trying to stuff his intestines back into his stomach. Mahoney's leg was drenched with blood.

"Such courage!" the colonel said, pointing his finger in the air. "Such élan! What a magnificent—"

A German bullet whacked the colonel on the cheek and blew away his jaw, mouth, and nose, spraying blood all over the street. The colonel stood for a second with his finger still in the air, then collapsed to the ground.

A tubby little medic ran on bow legs toward the colonel. He kneeled beside him, took one look, felt his pulse, and shook his head. "He's a goner," the medic said. Then he hopped toward the kid, who was hollering and screaming and hugging his steaming guts. The medic jabbed a needle into the kid's arm, and the kid relaxed.

The German tanks had formed their wedge and roared their engines as they moved forward, firing their cannons at the section of the barricade in front of them. They wanted to bull their way through the barricade and speed through town, but the anti-tank gunners had other plans. They fired at the mass of tanks and couldn't miss because the tanks were so close together. The ground shook with the violence of the explosions, and tanks farther back in the formation had to change direction to avoid hitting ruined tanks in front of them.

Mahoney loaded his bazooka by himself, put it on his shoulder, and aimed at the treads of the tank closest to him. He pulled the trigger, and the rocket swooshed out, landing inside the tanks's tracks and blowing them off their runners.

Mahoney turned to load his bazooka again and saw a grizzled old soldier behind him.

"I'll load it up for you, Sarge," the old soldier said.

Mahoney turned to the front again. Ruined tanks smoked and burned, and undamaged tanks tried to break through the barricades. The top hatch on one of the damaged tanks opened, and German tankers in black uniforms and berets jumped out. Mahoney dropped his bazooka, picked up the carbine, flicked it on automatic, held the butt against his shoulder, and pulled the trigger. Fire and lead spit out the barrel, and the German tankers dropped their submachine guns and spun through the air, spraying blood onto the charred hulk of their tank and the icy cobblestones.

Mahoney lifted the bazooka again. The old soldier behind him tapped his helmet. Mahoney aimed at the treads of a tank and fired, but his rocket bypassed the tank and crashed through a store window on the far side of the street, exploding and blowing yellow fire and chunks of debris into the street.

The German tanks kept coming, and the American soldiers in front of them scattered out of the way. The tanks pushed through the barricade and shifted into high gear. The old soldier tapped Mahoney's helmet, and Mahoney fired at the rear deck of one of the tanks. This time he didn't miss, and the tank disappeared in a cloud of smoke. A split second later an anti-tank shell hit the same tank and pulverized it. When the smoke had cleared, the tank had become a pile of junk.

"KRAUT SOLDIERS COMING!" somebody screamed.

Mahoney looked down the street and saw a horde of German soldiers advancing with fixed bayonets. The old soldier tapped Mahoney's helmet, and Mahoney aimed his bazooka into their midst. Pulling the trigger, he saw the projectile streak toward the Germans and plow down a number of them before hitting the pavement and exploding.

Americans fired BARs and anti-tank shells at the charging Germans, but they kept coming anyway. Mahoney fired one more bazooka shell at them, blowing a hole in their front rank, but the German soldiers who hadn't been killed or wounded didn't falter and charged down the boulevard at the Americans.

"FIX BAYONETS!" somebody yelled.

Mahoney looked around and saw an M-1 rifle lying next to a dead GI. He picked up the M-1 and stuck his bayonet on the end because an M-1 was a longer, heavier weapon than a carbine and more formidable in close quarters.

The Germans were quite close now, screaming and shouting and shaking their rifles and bayonets as they raced toward the barricades.

"FORWARD!" hollered an American officer, jumping over the barricade and charging toward the Germans. "FOLLOW ME!"

His bold gesture inspired the GIs. They leapt over the barricades and followed the officer although many of them never had seen him before in their lives.

Mahoney was one of the first over the barricade, bellowing like an elephant, enraged at the Germans for shooting him in the leg.

"GET THE COCKSUCKERS!" Mahoney screamed.

"SKIN THE FUCKERS ALIVE!" somebody else yelled.

The German soldiers and GIs came together in the middle of the street and fought for their lives. Bayonets clashed and rifle butts slammed against helmets. Limping on his left leg, Mahoney ran toward a German corporal who lunged at Mahoney with his rifle and bayonet. Mahoney didn't dodge or try to retreat backwards. He planted his left foot between the two feet of the German, parried the German's rifle and bayonet to the side, and delivered a horizontal buttstroke to the side of the German's head. He caved in the German's head, and the German's legs gave out underneath him.

Mahoney jumped over the German and drove his rifle and bayonet forward, smashing through the guard of another German soldier and burying his bayonet in the soldier's chest. The German's eyes rolled up into his head, and he sank to his knees. Mahoney tugged to free his bayonet, but it wouldn't come out of the German's chest. He pulled the trigger of the M-1, and the German's lungs and intestines blew apart, splattering Mahoney with blood and portions of the German's organs. Mahoney raised his gory bayonet, saw another German soldier, and leapt toward him, pushing his bayonet toward the German's stomach.

The German parried Mahoney's bayonet to the side and tried to slam Mahoney in the head with his rifle butt, but Mahoney ducked and brought his own rifle butt straight up, catching the German on the chin. The German's head snapped back, and Mahoney punched him in the stomach with his rifle butt, and then, as the German fell backwards, brought his bayonet down and slashed the German from neck to hip bone. The German shrieked horribly and dropped to his knees.

Mahoney kicked him in the face, and another German soldier jumped in front of Mahoney, trying to harpoon Mahoney's head with the end of his bayonet.

Mahoney sidestepped and feinted with his own bayonet. The German moved to parry Mahoney's bayonet, not realizing it was a feint, and Mahoney shoved his bayonet into the German's throat. Blood burbled out the German's nose and mouth as he fell to the ground.

Mahoney spun around and found himself face to face with an American soldier. They made a motion to charge each other, realized they were on the same side, grinned, and turned to look for more Germans. Mahoney saw a German officer facing the side, aiming his service pistol at a GI. Mahoney ran toward the officer and rammed his bayonet into the officer's left kidney. The officer screamed and fired wildly into the air as Mahoney pulled his bayonet out and banged the officer in the head with his rifle butt. The officer collapsed onto the street.

Mahoney stepped over him and a German rifle butt came crashing down out of the squirming melee in front of him. Mahoney flinched backwards and nearly dropped his rifle, but he managed to hang on and bang the German in the head with his rifle butt, but the German dodged at the last moment, and Mahoney only succeeded in knocking off the German's helmet.

The German had blond hair and classic Nordic features. He looked like a recruiting poster for the SS, but he wore an ordinary Wehrmacht uniform that was torn in a few places. He lunged at Mahoney with his bayonet, but Mahoney parried it out of the way. The German feinted, but he didn't fool Mahoney. You had to get up pretty early in the morning to fool Mahoney. Exasperated, the German soldier feinted again, but that was what Mahoney had thought he'd do. Mahoney shot his bayonet forward and rammed it up to the hilt in the German's chest. The German said *oof* and blood poured from his nose and mouth. Mahoney pulled his bayonet free and slammed the German's bare head with his rifle butt. The German's head cracked apart, and his blond hair became drenched with blood as he sagged to the ground.

Mahoney looked up and saw more Germans running toward him, followed by a sea of tanks.

"FALL BACK!" somebody shouted. "TAKE COVER!"

Mahoney stepped backwards, still fighting off Germans, as he and the other GIs retreated to their barricade.

SIX

Field Marshal Model frowned as he looked at the map in the trailer that was his mobile field headquarters. His panzer armies had struck deep into the American line, but few of them had attained the objectives designated for them at noon on the first day of the attack. The Americans were fighting with inexplicable bravery, and Model was becoming alarmed. He and everybody else in the German Army believed that the Americans had won all their previous battles due to their superior numbers and firepower, but in this offensive the Americans were both outnumbered and outgunned, and yet they hadn't panicked and fled as everyone thought they would. The Americans were fighting hard and retreating in an orderly fashion. In some outposts on the Schnee Eiffel, the Americans had fought to the last man.

The map showed the panzer armies making impressive progress, but Model knew better. They should have gone much farther than they had. If the Ardennes offensive was to succeed, the panzer armies would have to move faster.

His eyes fell on the town of Clervaux, one of the main problem areas in the advance. The town lay astride the principal road to the west, and the panzers were supposed to have passed through it at seven o'clock in the morning, but now it was one in the afternoon, and a small force of stubborn Americans were still holding out against a panzer division and two regiments of picked infantrymen.

He wondered what the latest news was on the situation in Clervaux. Turning to his radio operator, he said, "Get me General Manteuffel immediately!"

"Yes sir!"

The radio operator fiddled with dials and spoke into his microphone, as Model readjusted the monocle in his right eye and looked at the map. He was worried that Hitler would call and ask how things were progressing. Hitler and Jodl had planned every step of this offensive themselves, and they wouldn't be pleased if they knew it was falling behind schedule already.

"Sir, I have General Manteuffel for you," said the radio operator.

Model took two long strides, plucked the headset from the radio operator's hands, and put it on.

"Manteuffel?" he asked.

"Yes, sir."

"Do we have Clervaux yet?"

"No, sir."

Model made his voice stern. "When will we have it?"

"Before the end of the day, sir."

"You're aware that we were supposed to have had it early this morning?"

"Yes, sir. The Americans are giving us a lot of trouble. We've tried everything, including aerial bombing, but they're making us bleed for every inch of ground they give up. I haven't faced a foe like this since Stalingrad."

"The Fuehrer will be furious if Clervaux holds up the advance much longer. Your career may be in more danger right now than you realize. You were supposed to be in Bastogne by nightfall."

"I'm doing my best, sir," Manteuffel said testily. "If you don't think so, you may relieve me of command."

"It hasn't come to that yet," Model replied. "But it might. Get a move on."

"Yes, sir."

"Over and out."

Model returned the headset to his radio operator and walked back to his map table. The road from Clervaux, and indeed most of the roads in the Ardennes, led to Bastogne, the largest and most important city in the area. Unlike Clervaux, Bastogne could be bypassed geographically, but it could not be bypassed militarily because the garrison there would always be a threat to the rear of the German advance.

Bastogne would have to be taken if the offensive were to succeed.

Model placed his index finger on the city of Bastogne and set his jaw. Bastogne was the key to the entire offensive. If it were not taken soon, the offensive would collapse, and if the offensive collapsed, Germany would have no further chance of negotiating a peace settlement with the Western Allies.

How strange, Model thought, that such an out-of-the-way insignificant town should suddenly become so important to the future of Europe.

In Bastogne, General Troy Middleton ate a baloney sandwich while looking at his map table. He knew he was facing the greatest crisis of his long military career. Although still out of contact with most of his units, enough of them had got through to give him a hazy picture of catastrophic reversals all across the Eighth Corps front. He'd spoken with General Hodges two more times about the situation, but Hodges was imperturbable as always. The Fifth Corps was attacking the Roer dams in the north, and Hodges was reluctant to break off the attack because if the Germans blew those dams, they'd flood Holland and stop all the American armor and troops in the area. Hodges said it would be foolish to send the Fifth Corps south on the basis of the scanty information that Middleton had provided.

"It's probably just a little spoiling attack to divert our attention from somewhere else," Hodges had said.

But Middleton didn't think it was a little spoiling attack although he couldn't prove it. His instincts told him that something big was going on, and it appeared headed for Bastogne. He knew very well that if the Germans wanted to advance to the Meuse, they'd have to take Bastogne because it was the most important road and rail center in the region.

He placed his finger on the part of the map where Bastogne was located and bit off a piece of the baloney sandwich, wondering how long it would take for Hodges to send help to the embattled Eighth Corps.

SEVEN

The sun sets early in northern Europe in December, and at three-thirty in the afternoon, darkness was already falling on Clervaux. Mahoney lay in a cellar on a narrow sidestreet, firing a .30 caliber machine gun at German soldiers while at another window an anti-tank crew was ravaging German tanks.

Someone tapped Mahoney's shoulder, and Mahoney turned around. A young greasy faced medic wearing a white armband was standing there. "Sergeant," he said, "I think you'd better go back to the aid station and get that leg of yours taken care of."

Mahoney looked down at his leg, which was still oozing blood. His pantleg was like cardboard due to dried and frozen blood. "It's okay," he said.

"It doesn't look so good to me, Sergeant, and I don't have any more sulfa. It's liable to get infected, and then they'll have to cut if off. You can't expect a bleeding wound like that not to get infected sooner or later, and if you keep on losing blood, you're going to pass out before long."

Mahoney imagined himself in a bayonet fight, too weak to hold up his rifle because he'd lost too much blood. "Maybe you're right," he said. "Where's the aid station?"

"Just a few blocks from here, near regimental headquarters."

The medic gave Mahoney directions, and Mahoney tried to memorize them. He realized that his mind hadn't been working too keenly for the past hour or two, and he didn't know if it was because of the loss of blood or the brandy that he kept sipping whenever he got thirsty. He took his canteen from its case and had another sip while the medic was still talking to him.

"That smells like booze to me," the medic said, twitching his nose.

Mahoney held out the canteen. "Have some."

The medic took the canteen.

Mahoney looked around. "Somebody had better man this machine gun here because I got to go to the aid station."

Three riflemen moved toward the gun, keeping their heads low because German machine gun bullets were whizzing through the open windows. Mahoney snatched his canteen out of the medic's hands before he drained it dry, and just then, a German shell hit the side of the building. Chunks of plaster fell down from the ceiling. Mahoney waved his hands through the air to clear away the clouds of dust so that he could find the door. He passed through it and limped down a corridor to the rear of the building. He felt exhausted and was half-drunk from the brandy. Leaving the building through the rear door, he crossed a backyard, passed through an alley, and wound up on a street where no fighting was taking place. He followed the medic's directions, and as dusk fell on the city, he soon came to the firehouse that was the regimental headquarters. Next to the firehouse was a former bakery shop that was being used as a field hospital.

Mahoney walked inside the hospital and saw soldiers lying everywhere. Medics and doctors rushed about, trying to examine wounds and save lives, and to Mahoney's disappointment, all the nurses were gone. They must have been evacuated when the Germans got too close.

A medic walked up to Mahoney. "What's your problem, Sergeant?"

Mahoney pointed to his leg. "The medic up front told me I'd better get this looked at before it got infected."

"Can you stand on it all right?"

"How do you think I got here?"

"The bone probably isn't broken. Have a seat, and I'll get back to you."

The medic dashed off, and Mahoney looked for someplace to sit. All the wall space was already taken, so he limped a few steps and sat between two soldiers who were swathed in bandages. He took out a cigarette and lit it up.

"You got an extra one of those, buddy?"

Mahoney looked up and saw a GI with his arm in a sling.
"Sure."

The GI kneeled, and Mahoney gave him a cigarette and a light.

"How's it going out there?" the GI asked.

"The krauts have got about three-quarters of the town."

"Shit, I can't see why we don't give them the fucking town and leave."

Mahoney could have explained to the GI that in a war it wasn't a good practice to give up ground, but he didn't feel like making a speech. Instead, he puffed his cigarette and grunted. The GI took the hint and walked away. Mahoney closed his eyes and thought it would be nice to go to sleep in a nice warm bed someplace with clean sheets and a clean woman with big brown eyes like Madeleine.

"Hey, soldier!"

Mahoney opened his eyes and saw the medic.

"Come with me."

Mahoney rose and followed the medic across the room. He wasn't surprised that they'd called him right away because often the medics would treat first the men whom they could return to duty right away, instead of those who probably would never fight again.

Outside on the street, Captain Carlson, the officer with whom Mahoney had returned to Clervaux from the fight on the road earlier in the day, was walking toward the firehouse to speak with Colonel Knowland, the commanding officer of the Fifty-third Infantry Regiment in Clervaux.

Carlson was filthy, bedraggled, and greatly troubled. He carried his carbine at sling arms and looked at the sidewalk in front of him, trying to formulate the report that he intended to make to Colonel Knowland, whom he didn't know very well and who was supposed to be a holy terror.

He would have had more to worry about if he'd been aware of the three German soldiers in American uniforms watching him from the window of a building across the street. They were Lieutenant Gurtner and Sergeants Muller and Grieser, and Muller was aiming an M-1 rifle at Captain Carlson's head.

"Should I shoot him?" Muller asked.

Gurtner looked at Carlson through American binoculars. "No, he's only a captain. There's a colonel in that fire station. He's the one we want."

"Why don't we go in after him?" Grieser asked. "He's probably alone except for a few officers. All we have to do is open the door, toss in a hand grenade, and run away."

Lieutenant Gurtner wrinkled his forehead and thought for a few moments. "You know, that might work," he said. "Let's go."

The three Germans stood up and walked out of the room, heading for their jeep parked in a yard a few blocks away.

Meanwhile, Captain Carlson entered the firehouse and made his way to the conference room, knocking on the door.

"Come in!" said a voice inside.

Carlson took off his helmet, revealing straight light brown hair, and entered the conference room. Colonel Knowland and four of his aides stood around the map table, under a kerosene lamp. Carlson walked to Colonel Knowland and saluted.

"Sir," he said, "I hope you'll forgive this intrusion, but I have something very important to discuss with you."

Knowland scrutinized Carlson's features and recalled seeing him at a distance at parades, meetings, inspections, and similar impersonal situations. "What's on your mind, Captain?"

"Sir, I'm in the 112th Engineers, and as you know we're supposed to blow bridges and other installations so the Germans can't use them in the event that they take ground from us."

"I know what engineers are supposed to do," Knowland said with annoyance. "What's your problem?"

"The gasoline dump outside Liederveld, sir. I've been wondering if anybody's going to blow it."

The colonel wrinkled his forehead and looked at his aides. "Do any of you know?"

They shook their heads. The colonel turned to Captain Carlson again. "That's an engineering responsibility," he said. "Why haven't you asked Colonel Drake?"

"He was killed in action today, sir."

Colonel Knowland's face went loose. "Oh."

"You see, sir," said Carlson, "the whole battalion was rushed here to Clervaux early this morning. I don't know if anyone was designated to blow that dump if the Germans get close to it."

"Well," replied Colonel Knowland, "they're damn well going to get close to it. They'll have this town in a few more hours, and then there won't be anything between them and that gasoline dump. If they get their hands on that gas, they'll go all the way to the English Channel."

"That's what I was thinking, sir."

Colonel Knowland stood more erectly. "Captain, I think you'd better take some men and make sure that the gasoline dump doesn't fall into the hands of the Germans. Do you have the means to blow it up?"

"There are explosives and caps hidden on the site, sir."

"Maybe you'd better take some grenades or bazooka rockets along to make sure."

"I'll need transportation, sir."

"Take whatever you need. There's nothing more important in this sector than what you have to do." He scribbled an authorization on a sheet of paper. "Use this if you have any trouble."

"Yes, sir."

"Get going," Colonel Knowland said. "You can't let the Germans get that gas."

Captain Carlson took a step backwards and saluted. "Yes, sir."

"That should keep you going for a while," the doctor said to Mahoney. "Now all you need is a new pair of pants. Should I give you the name of my tailor?"

Mahoney grinned. "Naw, these'll be okay."

Mahoney pulled up his ragged, bloody pants, covering the fresh bandage the doctor had put on his wound. The doctor also had cleaned it out, put sulfa powder on, and sewn it up.

"You can return to duty now," the doctor said. "Just make sure you have somebody take the stitches out in a few days. Any medic can do it."

"Thanks Doc," Mahoney replied. "You wouldn't care for a shot of brandy by any chance, would you?"

The doctor's eyes lit up. "Wouldn't I?"

Mahoney handed him the canteen, and the doctor raised it to his lips. His Adam's apple jigged up and down, and Mahoney became alarmed.

"Whoa there," he said, grabbing the canteen and taking it back.

The doctor wiped his mouth with the back of his hand. "That was pretty good stuff."

"You're fucking right it is," Mahoney said. "That's why I want to keep some for myself."

Mahoney left the little room and entered the space where the seriously wounded soldiers lay on the floor. He lit a cigarette, walked to the door, and descended the steps to the street. His leg felt much better because the doctor had given him a shot to kill the pain while he put in the stitches. The thunder of explosions could be heard more clearly now that he was outside. It sounded as though a fierce battle was being fought only a few blocks away.

He passed the firehouse and heard somebody shout "Mahoney!" Spinning around, he saw Captain Carlson coming down the steps.

"Hiya, Captain," Mahoney said, reaching for his canteen. "Care for a drink?"

"A drink of what?"

"Brandy."

Captain Carlson narrowed his eyes and examined Mahoney's face. "Are you a little drunk, Mahoney?"

Mahoney burped. "Probably."

"Oh shit." Captain Carlson groaned. "Where are you headed?"

Mahoney pointed toward the fighting. "Back to the war."

"I need you for something," Captain Carlson said. "You're coming with me."

"Where to?"

"I don't have time to explain. Meanwhile, lay off the brandy. There's something important that must be done immediately, but first we need a jeep."

As if by magic, a jeep turned a corner and headed straight for them. In it were three GIs. Captain Carlson watched it as it stopped in front of the firehouse and the three GIs got out.

"Where are you men going?" Captain Carlson asked.

The three GIs became flustered because they were Gurtner, Muller, and Grieser, the German commandos.

"We were told to report for duty here," said Gurtner with a stutter in his voice.

"By who?"

"Our commanding officer."

"What branch are you?"

"Ordnance."

"Well, we don't need any Ordnance men around here," Captain Carlson said. "It's much too late for that. But I need some men to help me with something important. You're coming with me, and I'm requisitioning your jeep."

The three GIs looked at each other nervously. Mahoney thought there was something peculiar about them, but he'd been drinking so much brandy he thought everything was peculiar.

Finally Gurtner saluted. "Anything you say, sir."

"All of us can't fit in the jeep, so one of you will have to stay behind." Captain Carlson looked at Grieser. "You report to the front."

"Yes, sir."

Grieser walked off. Captain Carlson looked at his watch. "We don't have any time to waste. First we'll pick up some hand grenades."

"Where are we going, sir?" Gurtner asked.

"To the gas dumps at Liederveld. We've got to blow them up before the Germans get to them."

Gurtner and Muller looked at each other significantly, but Captain Carlson didn't notice because he was gazing into the distance and trying to figure out the best way to get to Liederveld. Mahoney noticed, but he didn't trust his perceptions because he was half in the bag. To steady himself, he took out his canteen and swallowed down some more brandy.

Captain Carlson looked at him crossly. "I think you'd better lighten up on that stuff, Sergeant."

"It takes away the pain in my leg, sir," Mahoney replied, neglecting to mention that it removed all other feeling too.

Carlson turned to Gurtner. "What's your name?"

"Stevens."

"How about you?" Carlson asked Muller.

"Bradford."

"Which one of you drives?"

Gurtner shot Muller a meaningful glance.

"I do," said Muller.

"Then start driving."

The four of them piled into the jeep. Captain Carlson sat next to Muller in front and Mahoney sprawled beside Gurtner in back. They drove a block to the armorer, and Captain Carlson went inside with Gurtner and Muller to get some hand grenades. Mahoney waited outside to make sure nobody stole the jeep.

He lay in the back seat, breathing heavily, his eyes half closed. The brandy was making him sleepy. He shouldn't have drunk so much of it, but it was too late now. The only thing to do was have another drink. Taking out his canteen again, he unscrewed the top and raised it to his lips. He took two swallows and it was empty.

"Son of a bitch," Mahoney said, screwing the top back on. A German artillery shell landed on the roof of a building across the street, and Mahoney thought, Gee, this stuff has a helluva kick.

Gurtner and Muller came out of the building with Captain Carlson behind them. Gurtner carried a crate of hand grenades, and Muller held some bandoliers of M-1 ammunition. Captain Carlson had a grenade launcher in his back pocket. They got into the jeep, and Gurtner drove away. An artillery shell landed twenty yards away, and they squinched their eyes as pieces of the cobblestones fell on their helmets. They heard the crackle of machine gun fire and ducked their heads.

"Get the hell out of here!" Captain Carlson said.

Gurtner slammed the gas pedal to the floor, and the jeep lurched forward. He hooked a left at the next corner, and Mahoney looked back to see German tanks rolling onto the street behind him. The Germans had captured nearly all of Clervaux and would be hot on their heels all the way to Liederveld.

Captain Carlson also turned around to look at the German tanks and noticed the worried expression on Mahoney's face.

"Think we'll make it, Sergeant?" he asked.
"We've got to make it, sir," Mahoney replied.

Mahoney slept as the jeep drove through the night. In the distance, to the rear of the jeep, the sky glowed red from the fires in Clervaux. Captain Carlson nervously looked at his watch. German tank columns weren't far behind, and he wouldn't have much time to blow up the gas tanks. He hoped the jeep wouldn't break down.

The front wheel hit a bump and jolted Mahoney into consciousness. He looked around and saw the night passing by. Fir trees were clothed in coats of snow, and there was no moon at all. His throat was parched, and he had a mild headache.

"You got some water in your canteen?" he asked Muller.

"Sure thing."

Muller unsnapped his canteen from its case and handed it to Mahoney, who took a swig.

"Thanks," Mahoney said, passing it back. "Where the fuck are we, anyway?"

Captain Carlson turned around. "We'll be there in a few more minutes. How do you feel?"

"Ready to roll."

The jeep threaded its way through the snow covered forest. It chugged up mountains and passed lakes covered with ice and snow.

"Take a right here," Captain Carlson told Gurtner.

Gurtner turned off the main road and continued over a winding road up the side of a mountain. He turned a corner, and the gas tanks came into view on top of a ridge. They were thirty feet high, painted green, and surrounded by a high barbed wire fence that a German tank could go through without even pausing.

The jeep approached the barbed wire gate and stopped. Captain Carlson jumped out and walked toward the guardhouse. A head appeared in the window of the guardhouse, and a sleepy faced soldier opened the door.

"Halt—who goes there?" the soldier said, fumbling with his rifle.

"It's Captain Carlson—open the goddamned gate!"

The soldier walked toward the latch. "Boy, am I glad to see you, sir. They left me here early this morning, and I haven't been relieved since. What the hell's going on?"

"The krauts are coming. After you open the gate, follow us in, and help out."

"Yes, sir!"

Captain Carlson returned to the jeep, and the soldier opened the gate. Gurtner drove the jeep through it, and Captain Carlson told him to stop near the first gasoline tank. The guard caught up with them, and everybody got out of the jeep. Gurtner moved toward Muller because he wanted to tell him how to proceed. Together they had to take the Americans by surprise and kill them, so they could save the precious gasoline for the advancing panzer armies.

"As soon as they turn their backs," Gurtner whispered, "shoot them."

Surreptitiously, Gurtner and Muller reached for their rifle straps. Ahead of them, Captain Carlson was pointing toward the gasoline tanks.

"I think," said Carlson, "that if we set explosives on every other gas tank, that ought to blow up all of them."

"Do we have enough time?" Mahoney asked.

"We'll have to hurry."

Carlson stepped off in the direction of the bunker where the explosives were hidden, and just then Mahoney heard the unmistakable snap of a rifle bolt. Instinctively he dropped to the ground as the night exploded. Rolling over, he saw Gurtner and Muller firing their rifles. Mahoney yanked a grenade from his lapel and pulled the pin. Bullets ripped into the ground near him, and he tossed the grenade. Gurtner and Muller saw it coming, stopped firing, goggled their eyes at it, and didn't know whether to run or try to grab it, as Mahoney rolled underneath the jeep.

The grenade exploded as Gurtner bent over to pick it up, and Muller ran away. Gurtner's arms and legs were blown off his body, and flying shrapnel hit Muller in the back. Mahoney aimed his rifle at Muller as Muller whimpered and writhed on the ground. Coming out from underneath the jeep, Mahoney walked cautiously to Muller, who was face down, reaching around with his hand to the hole in his back. Mahoney aimed at the back of Muller's head and pulled the trigger of his

M-1. Muller's head bounced like a basketball as the bullet smashed into it, and then Muller lay still, his head torn apart and blood surging from the wound in his back.

Mahoney glanced at the decapitated Gurtner, then moved toward the bodies of Captain Carlson and the guard. Kneeling beside Captain Carlson, Mahoney saw that he'd been shot twice in the back, but he still was alive, moaning softly.

"Captain Carlson?" Mahoney asked.

The captain didn't respond; evidently he was in a coma. He wouldn't be able to tell Mahoney where the explosives were. Mahoney turned to the guard and saw that he was still, the back of his field jacket covered with blood. Captain Carlson stopped moaning. Mahoney felt his pulse. The captain was dead.

Mahoney stood up and pushed his helmet to the back of his head. He was all alone, and somehow he had to blow the gas tanks before the Germans arrived. He ran several possible plans through his mind, but they all collided with each other, and he was immobilized by indecision.

In the distance he heard the sound of engines. Turning around, he saw lights from the German tank convoy. They weren't worried about an American air attack at night with the low cloud cover and were speeding toward the gasoline dumps.

Mahoney didn't know what it would take to blow up the gas tanks. He'd heard stories about the volatility of gasoline and wondered if the tanks would blow if he fired a bullet into them. But he didn't have time for experiments. He should have discussed all this stuff with Captain Carlson while they were driving here, instead of sleeping.

Mahoney noticed something that he hadn't paid any attention to before: the ridge that the oil tanks were on inclined down to a cliff that overhung the road below. The German tanks would have to use that road to reach the gasoline. He wondered if he could turn the gas loose and ignite it so that it would spill onto the German armored column. It seemed worth a try.

Mahoney ran toward the body of Gurtner, took out his bayonet, and ripped off Gurtner's pant legs. Tying them to his waist, he dashed to the jeep, lifted out the create of hand grenades, cradled it in his arms, and ran to the gasoline tank farthest from the edge of the cliff. He set down the crate, took out a grenade, and laid it on the ground. Then with his bayonet he cut a strip of cloth from Gurtner's pants. He wrapped the strip around the arm of the grenade and tied a knot. Pulling the pin, he placed the grenade under the gaosline tank's spigot.

Picking up the crate of grenades, he ran to the next tank and did the same thing, while in the distance the sound of the German armored column came closer. He placed armed, tied hand grenades under each of the twenty gasoline tanks on the ridge, then stuffed his pockets full of hand grenades and placed the rest of them near the tied grenade underneath the spigot of the last tank.

He turned the spigot on, and sweet smelling gasoline poured down onto the tied grenade and the crate beside it. Then he ran to the next tank and turned the spigot on it too. He ran as quickly as he could to every gasoline tank, turning on the spigots, as gasoline covered the ground around the base of the gas tanks. Mahoney ran back to Captain Carlson's body and nearly gagged from the stink of gas. He pulled the grenade launcher from Captain Carlson's back pocket, dropped it into his field jacket pocket, jumped into the jeep, started up the engine, and accelerated away.

He made a wide turn, skidded over the ice on the ridge, and headed for the road leading down the mountain. Looking at the lights from the German armored column, he could see that it was nearing the bottom of the mountain. Mahoney sped beneath the ridge and glanced up. The bottoms of the tanks were swimming in gasoline now, but it was only a small fraction of what the huge tanks still would contain by the time the German armored column showed up.

Mahoney drove five hundred yards past the ridge, braked, and drove his jeep into the bushes far enough so that it couldn't be seen from the road. Jumping out, he broke some branches off pine trees so he could cover the windshield and prevent it from reflecting light. Then he grabbed his rifle, slung it crossways on his back, and ran toward the woods beneath the side of the ridge. The snow was soft on top, but the layer before the last snowfall was a frozen crust, and he sped over it, dodging trees and bushes.

Finally, he came to the base of the incline. His heart

pounding and his headache becoming severe, he grabbed some tree branches and pulled himself up. He climbed, scrambled, and struggled to reach the top of the ridge. A few times he slipped and fell back, but he righted himself quickly and charged forward again. Branches slapped him in the face and made his cheeks bleed. Turning around, he saw the German convoy halfway up the mountain.

Mahoney gritted his teeth and redoubled his efforts. He knew that men's lives were hanging on his success in blowing the tanks. He thought that maybe he should have blown them when he had the chance, but he'd wanted not only to blow the tanks but also to ambush the German armored column with burning gasoline.

He gasped for breath and snot ran from his nose. His injured leg was hurting again, and he thought he was going to have a heart attack. "I never should have drunk all that brandy," he said to himself. "I wouldn't be having all this trouble if I hadn't drunk all that brandy."

He looked up and saw the top of the ridge. It was only twenty yards away, and he took heart because he thought he could cover twenty yards standing on his hands if he had to. Reaching for a branch for support, he broke it with his hand, and he fell backwards down the hill. His head fell in the snow, and his feet toppled over it.

He flailed wildly with his arms, trying to grab onto something, and finally connected with the trunk of a tree. He pulled himself erect and wiped the snow from his face. He'd lost his helmet, but he still had his wool cap on, the grenade launcher was in his pocket, and he hadn't lost his M-1.

Spitting a few pine needles out of his mouth, he resumed his climb. The armored column sounded awfully close, and he didn't dare look at it for fear it'd be too close for him to ambush. He pumped his legs and took huge gulps of air as he thrashed his way up the hill. He heard the tanks passing him on the left, and he wanted to cry with frustration, but still he kept going. If he hadn't fallen, he would have been ready for them, but he'd fucked up. Now all he could do was finish the job as quickly as he could.

Finally, with his hands numb from the cold and his face bleeding from scratches caused by branches, he reached the top of the ridge in time to see the German armored column rounding the bend and heading toward the gas tanks. Then, in the corner of his eye, he saw something that made his heart leap for joy.

Although the armored column was nearing the tanks, it was so long that a substantial portion of it still was underneath the ridge. Mahoney could destroy those tanks with burning gasoline if he acted quickly.

He yanked the grenade launcher out of his pocket and fastened it on the end of his M-1. He affixed a hand grenade to the launcher, inserted a shell into the chamber of the M-1, and let the bolt slide forward slowly.

He looked up and saw the *kubelwagen* leading the armored column stop near the bodies of Captain Carlson, the guard, and the three Germans disguised as GIs. Mahoney aimed at the big storage tank nearest him as a German officer waved his arms wildly; evidently he'd smelled the gas.

But it was too late for him and the rest of the Germans in the column. Mahoney pulled the trigger of his M-1, and its butt hit his shoulder like the kick of a mule. The grenade sailed through the air, and Mahoney watched it wide-eyed, praying it would hit the storage tank.

The grenade landed short in a puddle of gasoline, and exploded. The concussion caved in the side of the storage tank. A huge wave of burning gasoline surged from the tank, and the raging fire ran toward the tied up hand grenades. The cloth strips burned away and the handles snapped open. The grenades exploded one after the other, and flaming gasoline burst from the tanks and roared toward the ridge and the road on which the armored column was stalled. Horrified, the German tankers looked up to see an ocean of burning gasoline dropping toward them. The liquid fire engulfed them, and Mahoney could see German tankers in burning uniforms jumping from their tanks. The flames poured into their tanks and covered the ammunition.

One German tank exploded, sending its crew of flaming torches flying into the sky. Then another German tank blew up. It was followed by a third and a fourth. Mahoney watched, his mouth hanging open in awe of the damage he'd caused. Hundreds of tons of burning gasoline flowed down the cliff onto the tanks, and more of them exploded. Soldiers in burning uniforms ran in all directions, diving into the snow and rolling around.

Mahoney wished he had his platoon from Charlie Company with him because if he did, no German would leave the area alive. But Mahoney was alone, and he decided he'd better get the hell out of there before more Germans showed up to find out what was going on.

He removed the grenade launcher from the end of his rifle and dropped it into his pocket, snapping the pocket closed so that it wouldn't fall out if he fell again, because you never knew when you might need a good grenade launcher. Then he slung his rifle crossways on his back and slipped back from the ridge. He descended it carefully, holding onto branches so that he wouldn't slip and fall on his face. On the way down, he found his helmet and put it on. He noticed that not all of the armored column had been destroyed by the burning gasoline. Several of the tanks bringing up the rear had been able to pull back, out of harm's way. That meant Mahoney couldn't use his jeep because the krauts might see him. He'd have to reach safety on foot somehow, and he had no idea of where safety was.

He reached the bottom of the hill and looked back at the wreckage of tanks still burning on the road. The air was filled with bitter petroleum fumes tainted by the odor of roasting human flesh. Unslinging his rifle, he loaded in a fresh clip of ammunition and held the rifle in both his hands as he headed in the direction he figured was west.

EIGHT

Lieutenant General Omar Bradley, commander of the Twelfth Army Group, had been on the road all day and knew nothing of the German offensive. He arrived at SHAEF Headquarters in Versailles late in the evening for a conference with General Eisenhower and his aides on the infantry replacement problem caused by high casualty rates at the front. Bradley and Ike intended to work out a plan whereby non-infantry soldiers could be relieved of their duties and transferred to the rifle companies.

Ike greeted Bradley warmly. They swapped some amiable chitchat and then got down to business. Ike also knew nothing of the German offensive, due to disrupted communications and confusion in the Ardennes.

An aide submitted statistics about the number of soldiers available in non-combat arms for transfer to the front lines. Another aide thought that 20% of these soldiers could be made available for combat duty provided WACs could take up the slack. A discussion ensued over how to procure the WACs and how much havoc would be caused by having huge numbers of them stationed near sex starved GIs.

In the middle of the discussion, there was a knock on the door.

"Come in!" said Ike.

The door opened, and a colonel entered the conference room, carrying a sheet of paper. "Sir, I have an urgent message from First Army."

Ike held out his hand. "Give it here."

The colonel crossed the room and handed the paper to Ike, who put on his wire-rimmed glasses and read it. He furrowed his brow and laid down the paper on his desk, then took off his glasses. "Bad news," he said. "This morning the Germans launched attacks at five different points in the Eighth Corps sector of the First Army line."

General Bradley looked at his watch, and it was 2100 hours (nine in the evening). "They attacked this morning, and we're just finding out about it now?"

Ike nodded. "Evidently it's taken them a while to figure out what's going on. The report states that they've had problems with communications due to an extensive enemy bombardment."

Bradley turned down the corners of his mouth and shook his head. "I've been expecting something like this. The Germans evidently have mounted a few local attacks in the hopes that we'll halt Patton's offensive in the Saar and send him north to meet this threat."

Ike stared off into space for a few moments. "No, Brad, I don't think these are local attacks. It isn't logical for the Germans to launch local attacks at the weakest part of our line. They'd launch local attacks at strong points, but if they're hitting us where we're weakest it means they want some real estate or are trying to accomplish something else."

"Like what?"

"I don't know yet, but I don't want to wait around and do nothing until their intentions become clearer. Send Middleton two divisions just in case. You'll have to take at least one of them from Patton."

"He'll scream like hell."

"If he screams too much, just tell him that I'm running this war, not him."

Bradley left the conference room and walked down the hall to a vacant office. He sat behind the desk and told the operator to connect him with Patton's headquarters in Nancy.

After several minutes Patton came on the phone. He'd been having dinner with his niece, who was a Red Cross worker attached to his headquarters. "What's wrong, Brad?" he asked.

"We've got a problem, George," Bradley replied. "The Germans are attacking Troy Middleton."

There was silence on Patton's end for a few moments. "I had a feeling this was going to happen sooner or later," Patton said. "I've got some of my people on recon in Middleton's sector, and they've reported that he's got gaps in his line big enough to run an army through. I suppose you want me to go up there and do something about it?"

"Just send a division, George. That's all."

"But Brad," Patton pleaded, "that's only a goddamn spoiling attack up there. The Germans want you to do just what you're doing—weakening my offensive in the south. There's no major threat up there from the Germans. The problem is that I'm a major threat to them down here."

"I don't have time to discuss this with you, George," Bradley said. "I want you to send a division north right now, and that's an order."

Bradley imagined Patton turning red and gnashing his teeth on the other end.

"Yes, sir," Patton said.

Bradley broke off the connection and then told the operator to put him through to his own headquarters in Luxembourg City, so he could tell his chief of staff to have another division sent into the Ardennes from the Ninth Army in Holland.

While waiting for the call to go through, Bradley looked up and saw General Walter Bedell Smith, Ike's chief of staff, taking a seat on the edge of the desk.

"Beetle" Smith leaned toward Bradley. "Well," he said, "it looks like you've got what you wanted. You've been wishing for a long time that the Germans would come out of their holes and attack, so we could kill them easier."

Bradley nodded grimly. "I know," he replied, "but I didn't want them to attack in a spot where we don't have many soldiers."

It was after midnight at German Army Group G Headquarters on the east side of the Siegfried Line opposite Patton's Third Army. General Herman Balck, the commander of the army group, was sound asleep in his bed, when the phone on his night table rang.

He awoke with a start because he'd given orders that he wasn't to be disturbed at night unless it was a matter of the most extreme seriousness. Looking at the phone with dread, he wondered what had happened. Was Patton tearing up his front lines again?

He picked up the receiver and apprehensively held it next to his face. "Yes?"

"Sir," said the voice on the other end of the wire, "the Fuehrer would like to speak with you."

Balck sat bolt upright in bed and turned on the lamp. "Put him through," he said in a mild state of shock.

There was a bit of static, a loud click, and then the old familiar hoarse voice resounded inside Balck's ear. "Balck," Hitler said like a specter in the night, "are you there?"

"I'm here, my Fuehrer," Balck replied.

"I have good news for you, Balck. All your suffering and deprivations have not been in vain. Today I have launched a tremendous offensive against the Americans in the Ardennes, and I am pleased to report that the armies of the Reich have advanced deep into the interior of Belgium."

Balck shook his head and looked around the room because he thought he might be dreaming. "That's wonderful, my Fuehrer."

"Now I can tell you, Balck, why I've been unable to send you replacements these past few months. It was because I was building this huge reserve of men and tanks to attack the Americans. When I ordered you to hold Patton at all costs, it was because I wanted you to keep him out of my staging areas. But from this day on, Balck, we shall retreat no more. From now on, we march to victory!"

Balck was dumbfounded, and didn't know what to say.

"Can you hear me, Balck?"

"Yes, my Fuehrer. This is most welcome news!"

"I have saved the Reich once more," Hitler said. "Destiny has smiled upon me and tipped the scales in my favor. The direction of this war has changed dramatically in only one day. Victory is within my grasp. I'll see you in Paris by the first of the year, Balck. Take heart!"

"Yes, my Fuehrer, I certainly shall. Yes, indeed."

"That is all for now, Balck. You may return to bed with the knowledge that an entirely new era will dawn tomorrow. That is all. *Sieg Heil!*"

"Heil Hitler!" shouted Balck.

The phone went dead in Balck's ear. He returned it to its cradle and stared at the wall in front of him, trying to make sense of what his Fuehrer had told him. It was all so preposterous. Could it be true?

NINE

It was two o'clock in the morning somewhere east of Bastogne, and Mahoney trudged through a forest, wishing the stars were out so he could take a bearing and be sure he was heading in the right direction.

Mahoney had been having bad times ever since he left the gasoline dump. The temperature had dropped to twenty-two degrees; he was hungry, and he had a hangover. His leg was bothering him again, and he stank of gasoline.

At midnight he'd decided to get some sleep the way they had taught him in survival school at Fort Benning, Georgia. They'd said if you dug a little hollow in the snow, got into it, and covered yourself with snow, you would stay warm. Mahoney tried it, and it was like lying down inside a refrigerator with the cooling system turned all the way up. He'd stayed that way for a while waiting for the warmth to come, but it never did. He just kept getting colder and colder. Finally he climbed out of the hole, cursing the instructors at survival school at Fort Benning.

He decided the best way to stay warm was to keep moving. He didn't dare light a fire because it could be seen at night, and he didn't know if any Germans were around. Tomorrow he might be able to find a little cave or glen where he could make a fire and maybe cook a rabbit—although he had no idea of how to catch a rabbit.

He trudged through the snow, burping because his stomach had nothing in it but cold air. He tried not to think that he might get lost and die of starvation or exposure in the woods. He continued repeating to himself that he'd get back to the American lines somehow, although he didn't know where the American lines were.

He thought he'd been in the woods for centuries, but when

he looked at his two watches, he found out that only a half hour had elapsed since the last time he'd checked them. Assailed by rage and frustration, he dropped to his knees on the snow and fought to prevent himself from screaming. I can't take much more of this, he thought.

Mahoney clasped his hands together, closed his eyes, and prayed. He always turned to prayer in his most difficult situations because he'd been educated in Catholic schools in New York City and it was a reflex action to extreme hardship. "Oh Lord," he whispered, "if you get me out of this one, I'll give all my money to the church and I won't fuck girls anymore. I'll stop drinking, and I'll stop taking your name in vain. I also won't shoot any more craps."

Mahoney opened his eyes and saw a glimmer of light in the distance through the trees. Blinking, he looked again, and sure enough, something was there. Springing to his feet, he moved quickly through the snow, smashing branches out of his way, his eyes fixed on the light.

It became more distinct, and he thought it was a fire or a lantern far away. He continued to make his way through the woods, wondering what it was, and hoping that it wasn't a campfire surrounded by Germans.

Finally he came to the edge of the woods and looked down at a snow covered plain. A farmhouse sat on the plain, and the light was in one of the windows. Mahoney raised his binoculars and scanned the landscape. In the darkness, he could see no German vehicles or other signs of the Germans in the vicinity of the farmhouse, although there could be a few tanks parked on the side that he couldn't see.

He was tempted to sneak down to the farmhouse and take a look, but that wouldn't be prudent if there really were German vehicles parked on the other side. He'd have to take a long, circuitous route through the woods so he could see if anything was hidden on the blind side of the house. He groaned because he didn't feel up to it. He was tired and weak from loss of blood and lack of food, not to mention the brandy hangover. But he had to check out the other side of the house. Then, if Germans were there, he'd have to disappear into the woods again and continue heading in the direction he thought was east. If the farmhouse appeared to be free of Germans, he could sneak down and steal some food.

He moved through the woods to a position where he could see the blind side of the farmhouse. The vision of fat sausages hanging from the rafters of the farmhouse kept him going. There might even be some cheese and some freshly baked bread lying around.

Mahoney stomped around trees and bushes, thinking of fabulous meals. Maybe they had fresh eggs and coffee. Perhaps they'd butchered a pig lately and had some nice pork chops. Perhaps the farmer was a connoisseur of fine wine—although Mahoney had promised God he'd never drink again.

Finally he worked his way through the woods to a position where he could see the side of the farmhouse that had previously been hidden. He raised his binoculars and saw a barn on that side of the house, but no vehicles of any kind.

Mahoney smiled. Now he could go down and check the place out. He opened the bolt of his M-1 to make sure there was a round in the chamber because there might be some Germans there anyway. Scooping up some snow, he stuffed it into his mouth to relieve his thirst, and came out of the woods.

The field inclined gently downward to the farmhouse and barn. Mahoney moved along cautiously, his eyes scanning back and forth for signs of trouble, with one finger on the trigger of his M-1. It would be wonderful if food were down there along with a friendly farmer who'd let him sleep in the barn, but if there was trouble, Mahoney would be ready for it.

He approached the barn, stepping cautiously through the snow. He smelled animal manure and heard the rustle of hooves inside the barn. Although he was being careful and quiet, the animals with their incredible ears had heard him.

Then, suddenly, the sound of barking shattered the stillness. A brown and white dog that looked mostly collie rounded a corner and charged Mahoney, baring its fangs and drooling all over the snow.

Mahoney raised his rifle and prepared to shoot the dog if it made a move to bite him, but the dog kept its distance, barking and howling, trying to appear fearsome. Mahoney knew he was in trouble. He'd been discovered, and he couldn't run away because he'd be too easy to spot on the vast snow covered field.

"Sssshhhh," he said to the dog, "calm down you fucking bastard."

The dog kept barking and hopping around. Evidently it had been drilled into his head that his function on Earth was to sound the alarm if a stranger ever showed up on the farm.

The front door of the house opened, and a woman stepped onto the porch. She wore long skirts and a long wool coat, with a wool stocking cap on her head. "Do you speak French?" she called out to Mahoney in French.

"Yes, ma'am," he replied in that language.

"What do you want?"

"I'm awfully hungry, ma'am. I'd just like a little something to eat and then I'll be on my way."

The woman stepped down from the porch and walked toward him. Mahoney made a motion to meet her halfway, but the dog lunged at him.

"Get back, Ferdinand!" the woman shouted. "Come here!"

The dog laid back his ears, dropped his tail between his legs, and whined as he walked toward the woman. Mahoney didn't know whether to sling his rifle and show peaceful intentions or to keep it ready just in case. He decided to keep it ready just in case.

The woman came closer and stopped. She was in her late thirties or early forties with attractive features and a large bosom. Her hair beneath the stocking cap was medium blonde. She wrinkled her forehead and looked Mahoney over.

"Are you a deserter?" she asked.

"No, ma'am, "Mahoney replied. "I don't know if you know it or not, but the Germans have attacked Belgium. I've been cut off from my unit, and I'm trying to get to Bastogne."

She nodded. "Some German planes passed overhead yesterday, and we've heard bombardments in the distance. We thought something like that had happened."

"We?" Mahoney asked.

"My daughter and I." The woman turned around. "Cecille—it's all right!"

Mahoney looked at the farmhouse and noticed for the first time a female with a rifle in an upstairs window. The woman with the stocking cap faced him again. "My daughter and I have to be careful because sometimes soldiers don't know how to behave around women. But you appear to be a decent fellow. Come into the kitchen, and we'll get you some breakfast."

Mahoney slung his rifle. "That would be awfully nice of you, ma'am."

She smiled for the first time. "My name is Suzanne."

"I'm Mahoney."

They walked together toward the house, and Mahoney's mouth watered at the thought of the food.

"You're limping," she said. "What's wrong?"

"I have a wound in my leg, but it's been stitched up. I'll have to take the stitches out in another day or two."

"My husband is a doctor," the woman said. "He's away, but I know how to take out stitches."

"Well, they were just put in yesterday."

"It's too soon then. I'll have a look to make sure the wound's all right."

"Where's your husband?"

"He's in the Army. And my son too."

They entered the farmhouse, and Mahoney found himself in a kitchen with a kerosene lamp burning on the table. A blonde girl of eighteen, the one who must have been in the window upstairs, was feeding wood into an ornate cast iron cooking stove. She was slim with a cute, upturned nose and her hair combed back into a bun.

"Cecille," said the woman, "this is Mahoney, an American soldier."

The girl smiled. "Hello, Mahoney."

"Hi."

Her skin was creamy white, and Mahoney thought she was a living doll. Her mother took off her stocking cap and shook out her wavy hair. She was bigger than her daughter, the type often described as a handsome woman. In the light of the kerosene lamp, they could have passed as sisters.

Mahoney began to have carnal thoughts and closed his eyes because he recalled his promise to God a few hours ago that if he were saved, he wouldn't fuck women anymore. Please God, he prayed silently, please stop me from trying to get into the pants of these nice people here.

"Are you all right?" Suzanne asked.

Mahoney opened his eyes and smiled beatifically. "I was just making a little prayer, thanking the Lord for bringing me here, because I was afraid I would freeze to death or starve in the woods."

"You poor man," Suzanne said, pulling out a chair. "Cecille—make some coffee!"

"Yes, Mother."

Mahoney sat down and watched the women bustle through the kitchen. From cupboards, they took eggs, cheese, and sausages, and Mahoney recalled dreaming of these delicacies only a short while ago. It just goes to show you, Mahoney thought, that if you have faith in the Lord, He will always provide for you.

The women cooked the food and made coffee. The kitchen filled with the most delicious aromas Mahoney had ever smelled in his life. He offered the women cigarettes, but they both said they didn't smoke. Lighting one for himself, he puffed it contentedly.

Suzanne poured some hot water into a wash basin. "Come clean your hands," she said. "You'll have to take a bath after breakfast because you smell terrible."

Mahoney washed his hands in the basin and looked at the mirror on the wall, horrified by what he saw. He was filthy and scruffy and looked completely disreputable. Drying his hands on the towel, he could understand now why the women had been afraid of him at first. He looked worse than an escaped convict. He sat at the table, and the women placed platters of food in front of him.

"Help yourself," Suzanne said. "Don't wait for us."

Mahoney attacked the food, struggling heroically to keep himself under control. He shoveled eggs and sausages into his mouth, washed them down with hot coffee, and then gobbled the oven baked bread.

Sitting to his right, Suzanne smiled benevolently. "It's so nice to see a man with a good appetite," she said.

Mahoney's stomach filled, and he was able to behave with more decorum. He sat erect and used his knife and fork in the proper manner. He was even able to engage in a friendly discussion with the women, telling them where he was from and a few things about his life. In turn, he learned about them. Ordinarily they lived in Brussels, where Suzanne's husband had his practice, and they came to the farm in the summer for vacations. When food became scarce in the city, and the men of the household had to enter the army, it was decided that the women should move permanently to the farm, where they'd be certain of getting enough food to eat. They'd been here for several months and both were getting bored. Cecille missed her ballet classes, and Suzanne missed her friends.

"I've lost all the romantic notions I used to have about the country," Suzanne said wearily. "It's so dull out here. If you've seen one tree, you've seen them all."

When Mahoney's stomach was full, he leaned back in his chair and lit a cigarette. Suzanne and Cecille cleared off the table and did the dishes. Mahoney's eyes drooped sleepily, and he had a half hard-on from watching the women. Suzanne was buxom with an ample rear end and strong legs, whereas Cecille was like a fairy princess. If he had to choose between them in a whorehouse, he'd have to stop and really give it some thought.

"I think I'm falling asleep," Mahoney said. "Do you think it would be all right if I lied down in the barn?"

"The barn?" Suzanne said. "Don't be preposterous. We don't make our guests sleep in the barn. You shall sleep in the house here, but first you've got to take a bath." She looked at Cecille. "Go to the barn, and take care of your chores now, while I heat up some water for Sergeant Mahoney."

"Yes, Mother."

Cecille put on her coat, cast Mahoney a sidelong glance, and left the kitchen. Suzanne pumped the handle in the sink and drew some water, which she transferred to a big pot on the stove.

"You'll have to take your bath here in the kitchen," she said, "because it's the warmest room in the house. My daughter and I will wash your clothes, because they're absolutely filthy, and I'll get you some of my husband's things to wear. I also have one of his razors here, so you can shave."

She brought a big aluminum tub into the kitchen and set it on the floor. Then she ladled hot water from the stove to the tub.

"That looks like hard work," Mahoney said. "I can help you."

"Sit still. You'll only get in the way."

Finally, everything was ready. Suzanne brought Mahoney the razor and one of her husband's bathrobes.

"I'll leave you now," she said, "and go to help Cecille in the barn."

"Thank you, ma'am," Mahoney replied.

Suzanne put on her coat and hat and left the kitchen.

An hour later Mahoney sat at the kitchen table smoking a cigarette. He was shaved and bathed, and wore a thick robe. He'd emptied the filthy water into the sink and tossed a few more sticks of wood into the stove. He felt cozy and good, and soon he'd go to sleep.

"Hello!" Suzanne said from outside. "Are you finished?"

"Come on in!" Mahoney replied.

Suzanne and Cecille entered the kitchen, bringing cold air in with them. They both looked at him rather peculiarly, and Cecille said, "He looks nice without all the dirt and the growth of beard."

"Cecille!" said her mother.

Cecille blushed and took off her coat.

"Clean up the kitchen," Suzanne said, "while I show Mahoney to his bedroom and look at his wound."

"Yes, Mother."

Suzanne led Mahoney out of the kitchen and through a large living room with a stone fireplace and antlers hanging above it. A fire burned in the pit and heat radiated from the stone throughout the rest of the house. They climbed a flight of stairs, with Suzanne still leading the way and Mahoney's eyes level with her rear end. He wanted to reach up her dress and have a squeeze, but he knew that one shouldn't repay kindness with sneak attacks, and besides, he'd sworn that he wouldn't do that sort of thing to women anymore.

They entered a bedroom with flowers on the wallpaper. Mahoney looked out the window and could see snow falling again. On the dresser next to the chair were bandages, bottles of medicine, and medical implements.

"Sit down," she said.

"Yes, ma'am."

Mahoney sat on the chair. Suzanne fiddled with the instruments on the dresser. She took a pair of surgical scissors and knelt in front of Mahoney.

"Where is it?" she asked.

Mahoney pulled the bathrobe to the side and showed her the stitched gash. She bent forward and looked at it, probing gingerly with her fingers. "Does it hurt?"

"A little."

"I think it's too early to take these stitches out."

"Whatever you say, ma'am."

He looked down at her as she examined the wound, wiping away bits of gunk with a piece of gauze, and he felt all the energy in his body drifting down and filling up his dork, which rumbled about under the bathrobe. He became embarrassed because he knew she couldn't help but see it rising to life. She rested the palm of her hand on his hairy leg, and that made him hornier. Oh Lord, he thought, please don't let me grab this poor woman.

His dork got harder and finally the pesky thing leapt up and pushed its way through the opening in the bathrobe. Suzanne looked at it for a moment and whimpered. She squeezed his leg.

Mahoney reached down and pushed his stiff dork underneath the robe again. "Sorry about that," he said.

She sighed. "It's so lonely here in the country," she said in a strange, strangled voice.

Mahoney was breathing hard. "I know."

She snaked her hand into his bathrobe and wrapped her fingers around it. Mahoney thought he'd have an instant orgasm and shoot a hole in the ceiling.

"My God," she said, looking up at him with frightened eyes. "What am I doing?"

Mahoney wanted to say "We shouldn't," but instead he said, "Don't worry about it."

She looked down, brushed aside the robe, and brought his dork into the open where she could see it. "My husband's been gone for so long," she whispered.

"I'm sure you've had a real tough time," Mahoney told her.

She lowered her head and took the end of his dork into her mouth, moaning softly and making Mahoney curl his toes.

Mahoney looked up at the ceiling and thought, I tried my best, God, but you know the way things are.

After the blowjob, they had a quick screw on the bed, and then Suzanne went downstairs, and Mahoney fell into a deep, dreamless sleep. He felt as though he was drifting through black space for an eternity and then woke up late in the afternoon. Looking around, he didn't know where he was at first, but then he remembered everything. A man's clothes were folded nearby on a chair. Mahoney rolled out of bed, lit a cigarette, got dressed, and went downstairs.

The women were preparing dinner, and his uniform hung near the stove, drying after having been washed. Both of the women were polite and friendly, and he chatted with them as he lounged at the table in Suzanne's husband's pants and wool sweater. He asked if there was any danger of Germans coming to the farm, and Suzanne replied that the farm was far away from the main roads, and she didn't think it likely. Finally, dinner was served, and the main event was roast chicken.

"We killed it especially for you," Cecille said with a big smile that showed her beautiful white teeth.

"You shouldn't have done it for me," Mahoney protested as Suzanne placed the drumstick on his plate. "I'm really not worth it."

"Of course you are," Suzanne replied like an efficient housewife and mother. "Besides, if the Germans occupy Belgium again, they'll take all the chickens and other farm animals anyway, so we might as well enjoy them while we can."

They ate heartily, and Mahoney marvelled at the calm demeanor of Suzanne. She'd fucked and sucked him like a wildwoman earlier in the day, but now you'd never dream that she was capable of those things or that there was anything between him and her except the normal relationship between hostess and guest. You just can't trust any of them, Mahoney thought. They're all a bunch of fucking actresses.

Throughout the meal, Mahoney regaled them with true and semi-true army stories, and Cecille spoke of her ballet classes in Brussels. Suzanne talked about the happy times she'd had before the war, and they all had a marvelous time. After dinner they repaired to the living room and sat around the open fireplace, continuing their conversation, drinking wine, and laughing. Finally, it became dark, and Mahoney looked at his watch.

"I think I'd better go to bed early," he said, "because I'll want to get an early start in the morning."

"Don't be ridiculous!" Suzanne said. "You can't leave so soon. You're not even rested yet. Your wound isn't healed."

"I've got to return to duty," Mahoney said. "What I'm doing here could be considered desertion."

"Nonsense—you can stay one more day, and then before you leave I can remove your stitches. If you don't get them removed, you stand the chance of catching an infection."

"That's true," Mahoney replied. Actually he wouldn't mind staying another day and getting a little more of that good poontang, in addition to having his stitches removed. "Okay, I'll stay," he said.

Suzanne and Cecille appeared pleased. They all drank more wine, told more stories, and then at nine o'clock in the evening, they went upstairs and said good-night before entering their respective bedrooms and closing the doors.

Mahoney fell into a deep sleep, but this time he dreamed of New York. Outside, snow fell on the roof of the house and the nearby fields. Occasionally, the faint, muffled sound of artillery explosions wafted through the bedroom, but they didn't disturb Mahoney. His chest rose and fell evenly, and a faint smile was on his face. He rolled over onto his side and cuddled with his pillow. One would have thought that nothing could wake him up, but he was still a soldier, with a soldier's instincts, and when his doorknob turned, he opened his eyes.

In the dim light, he saw a wraith-like figure in white enter the bedroom, and he knew it was Suzanne. She closed the door and tiptoed to him, but as she drew closer, he was alarmed to see that she was Cecille. Mahoney closed one eye and pretended to be asleep.

She stood beside the bed and looked down at him for awhile. He could see her shivering underneath her gown. Then she turned and tiptoed toward the door. He'd thought she was going to crawl into bed with him, but evidently she hadn't the nerve. Mahoney wished she had the nerve. He didn't want her to go.

"Cecille?" he asked.

She stopped and looked back at him. "I'm sorry to disturb you," she stuttered, alarmed at being caught in his room.

"That's all right," he said soothingly. "I've been lying here thinking about you."

"You have?"

"Yes, and then when I opened my eyes, I saw you beside my bed. It was like a dream come true." He flung off the covers, got out of bed, and moved behind her, placing his hands on her shoulders. "You're so beautiful," he said, kissing her neck. "So lovely. How can a man fall asleep in the same house as you?"

She melted in his arms. "I've been thinking the same thing about you, but I was afraid to come to you, because you're—well—a guest here, and besides, I was afraid of you."

"Why?" he asked.

"Because you're so much older than I am. You seem so beyond me, like a heroic figure in an opera or a ballet, a warrior who came out of the night and walked into my heart."

Mahoney kissed her neck. He wanted to say something pretty and poetic, but he knew he never could top her remark. "Come to bed," he murmured in her ear.

He urged her toward the bed, and she didn't resist. He lay her down upon it and then lowered himself beside her, because he didn't want to get on top of her right away and perhaps scare her. Young girls were as skittish as colts. They changed their minds from moment to moment, and he didn't want this one to get away.

He didn't even grab her breast immediately, as he would have done with her mother. Instead, he held her thin waist and kissed her lips lightly, but she dug her fingers into his black hair, pressed her lissome body against his and opened her mouth, sucking his tongue inside.

Mahoney's brain became aflame with lust. She squirmed against him, scissoring her legs against his erection. He rolled her onto her back and picked up her nightie, running his fingers up her legs and making her tremble. He touched between her legs, feeling how soft and moist it was already, and she reached down and grabbed his joint.

"Oh, my goodness!" she said.

"What's wrong?"

"It's so big!"

"It's not that big."

"Yes, it is! It's enormous! It's too big for me!"

"No, it's not. Relax."

She manipulated it with her hand. "It's so incredible," she whispered.

He inserted his finger into her warm, slippery goodness and moved it around slowly. He realized that all women are magnificent, but there's nothing like a young girl. They're so sweet and loving, innocent and childlike, and crazy as hell.

She moaned into his ear and licked it with her pink tongue. He ran his finger in and out of her, and she relaxed beneath his ministrations, spreading her legs and sighing. Finally, Mahoney decided that the time had come for serious sexual relations. He crawled on top of her, held his dong in his hand, and rubbed it against those silken lips. She grabbed his hips with her hands and pulled him closer.

He slid it in slowly all the way to the hilt, and the poor child nearly fainted with pleasure.

"Are you all right?" he asked.

She nodded. He cupped her firm little buttocks in his hands, then pulled his hips back, and she raised her hips because she wanted to keep him inside her. When she could raise her hips no more and it appeared as though he was going to pull it out, he eased it back in again all the way and held her fanny firmly. She was marvelously tight, and he admitted to himself once again that there's nothing in the world like a young girl. The older ones were nice too because they generally knew more about these things, but there's nothing like a young girl to make your skin tingle and your heart sing.

He pumped her easily at first, and she met him stroke for stroke. She wrapped her ballerina legs around him, and he fastened his mouth on hers, drinking the nectar and eating the fruit. He struggled to prevent himself from going too wild and making the bed creak, but he worked her like a machine, making her come twice before letting himself blast off.

They didn't bother resting because neither of them was tired. He rolled her onto her belly, spread her legs, and slipped it into her again. He cupped one of her firm little breasts with one hand and rubbed his finger against her gumdrop with his other hand as he worked her, rolling around on her sweet little ass, making her come two more times but holding himself back this time for the grand finale that he'd planned for both of them.

He rolled onto his back and told her to sit on it.

"How?" she asked innocently, although by now he suspected that she'd done that before and every other weird thing that men and women do.

He showed her how to straddle him and helped her put it in. She rode up and down on it a few times and smiled, touching her lips to his.

"This is nice," she said.

"Go berserk," he told her.

She moved up and down and all around. He held both of her breasts in his hands and kneaded them, touching his fingers to her nipples, as she bounced about, moving her arms into exotic ballerina arabesques, leaning her body this way and that, raising her chin high in the air as if she was onstage as the Swan Queen.

His dam broke, and he gushed inside her, as she went into convulsions, collapsing on top of him and moaning softly. Gradually both of them became still, gasping for air, their bodies covered with perspiration.

Mahoney was exhausted and drenched with pleasure, but even at that moment his soldier's instincts had not deserted him, and he heard the doorknob turning.

"It's your mother!" he whispered, pushing her off him.

Quick as a gazelle, Cecille jumped out of bed and dashed into the closet. The door to the bedroom opened all the way. "Who's there?" Mahoney said.

"Ssshhhh," replied Suzanne, closing the door behind her. "It's only me."

"Oh my goodness!" he said. "You scared me! I was having a nightmare, and I'm covered with sweat!"

"So you are," she replied, touching his arm and getting into bed with him. "What were you having a nightmare about?"

"The war," Mahoney replied.

"Ah, you poor soldiers," she said consolingly. "You have such difficult lives."

She reached for his dingle, but that was the last thing he wanted her to touch. He took her wrist and guided it to his shoulder. They embraced and kissed.

"It's like a furnace in this bed," she said.

Mahoney kissed her lips and inserted his tongue into her mouth. She closed her eyes and moaned softly, but Mahoney's eyes were open, looking past Suzanne's ear to the closet. He saw the door open and Cecille slip out like a phantom of the night. She flew toward the bedroom door and left silently. Mahoney rolled Suzanne onto her back and ran his fingers up her thigh. She spread her legs obligingly, and her tongue in his mouth flicked around expertly, heightening his ardor.

"Do it to me now," she whispered.

Mahoney crawled on top of her, and after a while he had to admit that although young girls have nice firm bodies and lots of enthusiasm, the older ones ultimately give you the best sex because of their greater sophistication and finesse.

They wrestled with each other for an hour, and then Suzanne returned to her bedroom, and Mahoney collapsed into a deep slumber.

TEN

The next morning at breakfast, it was as though the events of the night before had never happened. The three of them carried on conversations like civilized, courteous people instead of total sex degenerates. After breakfast, Mahoney went to the barn with Cecille to help her with her chores, and wound up screwing her on a haystack. In the a... Suzanne looked at Mahoney's wound and gave him ano... blowjob.

That night Suzanne visited him again but not Cecille, who evidently was afraid she might run into her mother.

The next morning Mahoney was scheduled to leave. Suzanne removed his stitches, and he put on his uniform. She told him how to get to Bastogne, and they had breakfast, during which Mahoney had to admit to himself that if they were good actresses, he was a good actor, and if they couldn't be trusted, neither could he.

After breakfast the women stuffed his pockets, with bread, cheese, and sausages.

"I wish you could stay longer," Suzanne said. "We could use a man on the farm."

"I have to return to duty," Mahoney replied. "I'm no deserter."

She looked into his eyes. "Good luck, Sergeant."

"Thank you for everything, ma'am."

Then it was Cecille's turn. "I'll pray for you, Sergeant," she said.

"I'll pray for you too."

The women had tears in their eyes as they waved goodbye. Mahoney slung his rifle over his shoulder and marched through the gray dawn toward the woods.

The resort town of Spa was the scene of tumultuous frenzy, as its residents packed hastily and fled west. The streets were crowded with civilian and military vehicles, people on bicycles, and horses pulling overloaded wagons. Children cried, and adults had panic on their faces. In the distance, the ominous sounds of battle drew closer.

First Army headquarters was located in the Hotel Brittanica, and General Courtney Hodges was sitting at his desk, when the door burst open and General "Lightning Joe" Collins entered.

"Sir," he said, "I think it's time that you got out of here!"

Hodges was from Georgia and had the courtly manners of a southern aristocrat. "Have a seat," he drawled.

Lightning Joe was too excited to sit. "Sir, the enemy is getting awfully close!"

"I still have a few more things to do."

Hodges sat calmly and signed orders. His divisions attacking the Roer dams would turn south and hit the Germans in flank. The 101st Airborne was on its way to Bastogne. The Eighty-second Airborne would bolster the defense at Wiltz. But the picture of the German attack still wasn't clear. All he knew was that the Germans had broken through the Ghost Front as if it had been paper.

"Sir," Lightning Joe said, trying to keep his voice calm, "the Germans are only a mile away."

"Relax."

Hodges read more dispatches, and Lightning Joe continued to fidget. Hodges had seen a great deal of war, and nothing fazed him any more. He continued working until the Germans arrived on the outskirts of town, and then he calmly strapped on his helmet, walked downstairs, got into his jeep, and was driven away.

Mahoney made his way through the woods toward Bastogne. Suzanne had told him it was only about fifteen miles away, and he hoped to arrive sometime before tomorrow morning. She'd given him a road map of the area and her husband's compass, which was a more sophisticated one than those issued by the U.S. Army. Mahoney was confident that he'd make it.

At noon he sat beneath a birch tree and ate some bread, cheese, and sausage, washing it down with the wine that Suzanne had poured into his canteen. Mahoney felt as though Lady Luck was smiling on him and nothing could go wrong. The sounds of battle were far away. He suspected that the Americans had pushed the Germans back by now. He still had no idea of how widespread the German attack was.

After lunch, he stood and moved out again. He trudged through forests, across valleys, and up the sides of steep hills. Whenever he heard fighting, he circled around it and kept going. At dusk, he checked his map and compass, then continued in the direction of Bastogne.

He continued to move throughout the night because he felt

energetic and saw no point in stopping if he didn't have to. Every hour he checked his compass to make sure he was on course. The temperature dropped to twenty degrees, but he was full of calories, and his constant motion kept him warm.

At dawn he was on top of a high hill and surprised to see a village below. Checking his map, he saw numerous villages scattered throughout the area, and it could be any one of them. He looked through his binoculars and saw American jeeps and trucks in the town. Smiling, he realized that he'd bypassed all the fighting and now had made it back to safety. His worries were over.

Immensely pleased with himself, he descended the hill and approached the village. Two sentries came out of a doorway and challenged him.

"Listen," Mahoney said, "I've been trapped behind enemy lines for the past few days, and I don't know what the password is."

"Yeah, sure," said one sentry, holding his rifle on Mahoney.

The other sentry spoke into his walkie-talkie, then let it hang from the strap around his neck and aimed his rifle at Mahoney. The two sentries eyed him suspiciously. He knew they thought he was a German spy, and he probably would have thought the same of them if they showed up without knowing the password.

A jeep arrived with a sergeant in the passenger seat. The sergeant got out and walked toward Mahoney and the sentries. The sergeant looked at Mahoney as if he wanted to put him against a firing squad right away.

One of the sentries reported that Mahoney didn't know the password.

"That's right," Mahoney said. "I was cut off behind enemy lines, and I've been wandering around in the woods for a couple of days."

The sergeant looked at Mahoney's clean uniform and recently shaved face.

"You don't look like you've been in the woods for a few days."

"I spent some time in a farmhouse and got cleaned up."

The sergeant took out his .45 and pointed it at Mahoney's nose. "I think you'd better come with me."

Mahoney decided not to argue because he didn't think it

would get him anywhere. He gave up his rifle and marched to the jeep, getting into the rear seat. The sergeant held his .45 on Mahoney as the Pfc behind the wheel drove them to a building in the town.

Here I go again, Mahoney thought as he entered the building, expecting to be locked up again. He was taken down a hallway and into the office of a first lieutenant with curly blond hair and high cheekbones. On his collar was the insignia of the Signal Corps. The sergeant explained how Mahoney had shown up on the outskirts of town and didn't know the password.

The officer told Mahoney to sit down and proceeded to interrogate him. Mahoney stated his name, rank, and unit. He explained what had happened to him during the past few days, leaving out the bit about his arrest in Clervaux and the juicy details of his stay with Suzanne and Cecille.

"Unfortunately," said the officer, "I can't check your story because I don't have communication with Bastogne. You look and sound like an American, but so do the Germans who've infiltrated."

Mahoney nodded. "I know. I've run into some of them myself, and they fooled me."

"Sir," said the sergeant, "why don't we ask him some questions that any American would know?"

"We've been advised," the officer replied, "that the Germans have studied American culture and know pretty much what we do."

"Let me try, sir."

The officer nodded his assent, and the sergeant looked at Mahoney. "Who's married to Betty Grable?"

Mahoney groaned, because he'd never been very interested in the private lives of the stars. "Gee," he said, "I don't know."

Everybody looked at him suspiciously, and Mahoney knew his goose was cooked.

Mahoney shrugged. "I haven't had much time to read about stuff like that."

The sergeant looked at him coldly. "It's Harry James."

The first lieutenant was surprised. "I thought it was Artie Shaw?"

"Naw, Artie Shaw is married to Rita Hayworth."

The corporal standing guard at the door took a step into the room. "You're both wrong," he said. "Tommy Dorsey is married to Betty Grable."

"No he's not!" said the sergeant.

"He is too!"

The lieutenant raised his hand. "Calm down."

There was frenzied knocking on the door, and everybody looked at it.

"Come in!" said the lieutenant.

The door flew open and a Pfc ran into the room. "Sir!" he said, his face pale with terror. "The Germans are in town!"

The lieutenant shot to his feet. "What!" He dashed to the window and looked into the street. A column of German tanks rolled down the main street of the village, and hanging onto each tank were German infantry soldiers.

"My God!" said the lieutenant, becoming as pale as the Pfc.

Mahoney and the sergeant crowded around him and looked. Mahoney was surprised that none of the Americans in town had shot at the Germans yet, but he remembered that he was with a Signal Corps outfit, and fighting wasn't their game.

"What'll we do, sir?" asked the sergeant.

"I don't know."

Mahoney turned to the lieutenant. "How many men do you have in town?"

"Twenty-six."

Mahoney grunted. There was no point in taking on a tank column with twenty-six Signal Corpsmen. The only thing to do was flee.

"I'm getting out of here," he said, turning toward the door.

The sergeant pointed his .45 at him. "Oh no you don't!"

Mahoney glowered at him. "The krauts are here, asshole. The only thing to do is run for the hills."

"Yeah, but you may be one of them krauts yourself!"

Heavy footsteps pounded through the corridor outside. The door was flung open and five German soldiers wearing the uniforms of the Waffen SS charged into the room. The sergeant dropped his .45. An SS sergeant smiled superciliously and indicated with a hand motion that he wanted them to go outside.

They held their hands in the air and left the room. Mahoney cursed the stupid American sergeant for holding him up and then cursed himself for not bypassing the town.

They were herded outside with the other GIs. The street was swarming with SS men and tanks. Mahoney still hadn't heard a shot. The signalmen were surrendering without a fight.

Mahoney was disturbed because he had been captured so easily. He'd been a combat soldier for more than two years and always thought he knew how to take care of himself. If ever he would be taken prisoner, he thought it would happen only after he had put up a terrific fight, but instead, he was standing in the only street of a village whose name he didn't know, with a bunch of frightened signalmen, facing the gun barrels of SS soldiers with expressions of contempt on their faces, and it all had happened so quickly that he didn't have time to do anything.

He looked at the sergeant who'd taken him prisoner and wanted to strangle the stupid son of a bitch. The sergeant stood near the lieutenant, and Mahoney wanted to hate him too, but then sighed and realized they were only rear echelon soldiers who didn't know anything about war. If they'd had a real combat soldier for a leader, they might have been molded into a worthwhile fighting force, but their lieutenant was a rear echelon soldier too.

An SS captain approached them. "All right you men," he said in a thick German accent, "follow me!"

He led them between two buildings to a grassy field, then told them to halt and stand easy. Mahoney wondered what was going on. He wanted to smoke a cigarette but didn't dare reach into his pocket. A dozen SS men stood in a line, holding their rifles and machine guns. They laughed and joked with each other, and Mahoney figured everything was all right.

Then he saw the SS captain take out his service pistol, point it toward the ground, and work the mechanism that pushed a round into the chamber.

Uh-oh, Mahoney thought.

The GIs stood around and talked, paying little attention to the captain loading his pistol or the SS soldiers raising their rifles and submachine guns. Cold fear seized Mahoney, because he had a good idea of what was going to happen, but there was nothing he could do about it.

The captain raised his pistol and fired pointblank at the back of the GI in front of him. The explosion echoed across the field, and the GI slumped to the ground. The other GIs turned around to see what had happened, and the SS men with submachine guns and rifles opened fire on them.

Mahoney dove to the ground and lay still as bullets whistled through the air above him. The GIs screamed and bellowed in pain as the bullets sliced through them. They fell to the ground and spurted blood, and those who hadn't been hit in the first volley tried to run, but they didn't get far. The SS men continued firing and cut them down.

In a few seconds everything was still. Mahoney lay under two GIs who had fallen on top of him and whose blood soaked into his uniform. One of them was moaning and twitching, and Mahoney wished the GI would die and get it over with before he attracted the attention of the SS men.

Mahoney heard random gunshots. Opening his eye a crack, he saw SS men bending over GIs and shooting them in the head. Oh my God, Mahoney thought, closing his eye again. It's all over for me.

He didn't know whether to get up and make a run for it, or charge the SS men with his bare hands and die fighting like a soldier. Then, a little voice in his ear told him to lay still and maybe the SS men wouldn't disturb him. Blood from one of the GIs lying on top of him dripped onto his face, and he could feel it roll down his cheek. The other GI on top of him jerked convulsively. The footsteps of SS men came closer, and Mahoney heard one of them stop inches away from him. Mahoney held his breath and hoped the SS man wouldn't shoot him. A few moments of unbearable tension passed, and then a shot rang out. At first Mahoney thought his head had been shot away, but then he felt the GI on top of him jolt violently. The SS man walked away. He must have shot the GI who had been moaning and twitching because the GI wasn't doing it anymore.

Mahoney heard more shots. SS men were polishing off all the GIs who weren't dead. Mahoney knew now that he must never let himself be taken prisoner by the Germans if he ever got out of the mess he was in. It was better to die like a soldier with a gun in your hand than be slaughtered like cattle in a field.

The shooting stopped, and Mahoney heard the SS men talking as they stepped over bodies and moved in the direction of the street.

"What a bunch of disgusting cowards this bunch was," said one of the SS men.

"Yes, they were quite different from the ones we fought yesterday."

"Let's go!" said a voice that Mahoney recognized as belonging to the SS captain. "We must get moving again!"

The SS men marched away, but Mahoney continued to lie still. The icy December wind whipped across the field, and Mahoney felt blood freezing on his cheek, but still he didn't move. He tried to think of other things: the streets of New York in the summertime, basic training at Fort Dix.

The engines of tanks and armored personnel carriers started up on the street, and he heard them head west toward Bastogne. The sound of engines grew fainter. Finally he couldn't hear them at all. The field was still except for branches rustling in the wind. He was still afraid to move because SS men might have been left behind in the town. He'd have to wait until night to slip away.

He estimated that it was not more than seven or eight o'clock in the morning. It was going to be a long and horrible day, lying underneath dead GIs. He thought he might get frostbite from lying still, but that was better than a bullet in the brain. To keep from going insane, he'd have to think of optimistic possibilities.

Mahoney lost track of time. He didn't know if an hour had passed or only five minutes. Then he heard voices. Someone was coming. He opened one eye but couldn't see anything. Panic swept over him. Maybe some Germans were coming to bury the American dead!

He tried to think of what to do. If they were Germans, he'd have to make a break for it now while he still had the chance. If they weren't Germans, it wouldn't matter what he did. But on the other hand, what if they were Germans just passing through? If he remained still, they might go away, but if he moved, he'd get that bullet in the head.

The voices weren't very close yet, and he thought he might

permit himself to move and get a better look. Slowly and imperceptibly, he moved his head in the direction of the voices. It took a long time, but finally he saw civilians coming across the fields from the forest in the distance. Now he realized what must have happened. The townspeople fled when they saw soldiers coming to town and now were returning because they thought all the soldiers had left. He hoped they were right.

The villagers approached the dead GIs with horror and solemnity. The women held their fists in front of their mouths, and the men appeared to be in a state of shock.

"The swine," said one of the villagers, and Mahoney wondered if he was referring to the Germans or the dead Americans.

"Only the Boche would do such a thing," replied someone else, and now Mahoney knew whose side they were on.

He pushed the dead soldiers off him and tried to rise. The women screamed and ran, while their husbands and brothers were frozen to the ground with terror. Mahoney stood unsteadily, and everybody looked at him as if he was a ghost.

"I pretended to be dead," he explained, "They didn't get me."

Then in the corner of his eye, he saw another GI stagger to his feet. Again the women screamed, and Mahoney realized he wasn't the only survivor.

The other GI was a skinny soldier with a long sorrowful face and wire-rimmed glasses that he was adjusting on his nose with trembling hands. Mahoney walked over to him, as the villagers crowded around.

The two GIs stared at each other. Mahoney held out his hand. "What's your name?"

"Dunphy," said the soldier.

"I'm Mahoney."

They smiled at each other and shook hands, grateful that they had been spared.

"What's your rank, Dunphy?" Mahoney asked.

"I'm a private. How about you?"

"I'm a master sergeant."

Dunphy nodded. Now he knew who was boss. Mahoney turned to the villagers. "Does this place have a mayor?"

Everybody pointed to a stout man with a white mustache, who stepped forward. "I am the mayor of Stembelot."

"Sir," said Mahoney, "we'll need civilian clothes so that we can get back to our lines."

The old man nodded. "You shall have whatever you need."

ELEVEN

General Dwight D. Eisenhower, in a bulletproof car, was driven into the French city of Verdun. His car was in the middle of an MP convoy, and everyone was on the alert, because G-2 believed that German commando teams were roaming loose behind the American lines, looking for Ike so that they could kill him.

Ike believed the reports were exaggerated, but he had other things to worry about. Last night, after analyzing all the information available to him, he had been forced to conclude that the Germans had launched an all-out offensive against his First Army.

Hitler and his high command believed it would take a week for the Western Allies to reach this conclusion, but Ike had come to it in only three days.

Ike had scheduled a meeting in Verdun for all his top commanders, and now, finally, his car stopped in front of the old castle where the meeting was to take place. Surrounded by MPs with Thompson submachine guns held ready, Ike entered the castle and made his way to the conference room. All the brass came to attention when he entered, and he told them to stand at ease. Aides took his coat and helmet, and he advanced to the conference table, glancing at the troubled, unhappy faces. Only one face appeared confident, and it belonged to Lieutenant General George S. Patton, Jr.

Ike stood at the conference table and rested his fists upon

it. "Gentlemen," he said, "the present situation is to be regarded as one of opportunity for us and not of disaster. From now on there will be only cheerful faces at this conference table."

Patton grinned and puffed out his chest. "Hell," he said, "we ought to let the bastards go all the way to Paris, and then, when they've extended themselves to their limits, cut them off and chew them up!"

Everybody smiled at the brash and irrepressible Patton, but they all thought he really didn't mean what he said. However, they were wrong. Patton was willing and even anxious to do just that because he liked bold, unexpected moves and sweeping strategies.

Ike was much more practical. "No," he replied, "we're not going to let them cross the Meuse. We'll stop them where they are, but first we've got to take some pressure off the First Army." Ike turned to Patton. "George," he said, "I want you to go to Belgium and attack the Germans in force. How soon can you get moving?"

The room was silent because everyone expected Patton to explode with anger. They all knew he was in the middle of his Saar campaign and that he wouldn't want to break it off.

But Patton only said, "Immediately."

Ike blinked. "You mean today?"

"I mean as soon as you're finished with me here."

Ike became annoyed because he knew it could take a week or more for Patton to pull back his army, turn it north, and advance two hundred miles into Belgium. General Bradley noticed Ike's anger and thought he'd better say something.

"George," he said, "exactly how long will it take for you to actually engage the Germans in Belgium?"

Patton looked him in the eye. "In forty-eight hours with three divisions: the Fourth Armored, the Twenty-sixth, and the Hammerheads."

Ike couldn't take it anymore. "Don't be fatuous!" he snapped.

Patton turned to him. "I'll get there on time."

The officers in the room murmured. Some thought Patton could do it, and others figured he was bragging as usual. They didn't know that Patton had anticipated Ike's order and had set his staff to work on the move north before he'd come to Verdun. One code word on the telephone to his chief of staff would be sufficient to put the three divisions mentioned into motion.

Patton enjoyed the consternation he'd caused. He lit up a stogie and pointed to the map, which showed a big German bulge into Belgium. "Gentlemen," he said, "this time the krauts have put their heads into a big goddamned meat grinder, and I've got my hand on the switch."

Even Ike became infected by his confidence. "All right, George," he said with a smile. "I'll expect you to attack no earlier than the 22nd, and no later than the 23rd."

"Yes sir," Patton replied. "I'll hit them on schedule, and I'll be in Bastogne by Christmas just as sure as I'm standing in front of you right now."

The meeting continued. Ike told General Devers to move up elements of his Ninth Army to cover the hole Patton's Third Army would leave after he pulled out. Then he ordered Hodges to deploy the First Army so that it could attack the northern flank of the Bulge. Several other secondary matters were disposed of. Finally the meeting was adjourned.

Patton pounced on the nearest telephone and called his headquarters in Nancy. When his chief of staff came on the phone, Patton spoke the code word that would pull his three divisions off the line and send them north into Belgium. When Patton hung up, he turned around and saw Ike standing beside him.

Ike pointed to the new fifth star on his epaulette and grinned. "You know, George," he said. "I don't know why, but every time I get promoted, I also get attacked."

Patton winked. "That's right," he replied, "and every time you get attacked I'm the one who has to bail you out."

Meanwhile, the 101st Airborne Division, known as the Screaming Eagles because of the eagle depicted on their shoulder patches, arrived in Bastogne under the temporary command of Brigadier General Anthony McAuliffe. The division's usual commander, General Maxwell Taylor, was in Washington D.C. for conferences in the War Department.

McAuliffe was the division's artillery officer, a stocky dark haired man who tended to be economical with words. The city was in a state of chaos when he arrived, as civilians were trying to move back to safety, and the Screaming Eagles occupied the city. McAuliffe took over the headquarters vacated the day before by General Troy Middleton and the Eighth Corps staff, and the first thing he did was hold a meeting to determine what the situation was in the area.

Reports indicated that German armored units were heading toward Bastogne at top speed on the three roads that led into town from the east. McAuliffe thought the matter over quickly and decided to send three combat commands out to cover the three roads and attempt to block the Germans for awhile.

He knew he couldn't hold them back for long, but he thought he could hold them long enough for help to arrive.

Eight miles to the east, General Fritz Bayerlein was leading the famous Panzer Lehr Division through a thick fog toward Bastogne. He'd been told by his commanding officer, General Heinrich von Luttwitz, that Bastogne had to be taken immediately at all costs, "otherwise it would remain as an abscess on the German main lines of communication."

Bayerlein rode in an armored half-track, and behind him were fifteen tanks and four companies of infantry in halftracks. The rest of the Lehr Division was advancing toward Bastogne from other directions.

Bayerlein was a skilled panzer leader and had been Rommel's chief of staff in the Afrika Corps. He became commander of the Afrika Corps following Rommel's departure, and after the final debacle in North Africa, he was appointed to lead the Lehr Division, which had been formed from panzer units that demonstrated the latest blitzkrieg techniques to trainees, politicians, military brass, etc. It had taken severe losses since the Allied landings on Normandy beach, but had been brought to full strength for the Ardennes Offensive.

Now, in the darkening afternoon of December 19, Bayerlein peered into the fog and began to feel apprehensive about what lay ahead. He couldn't see much and thought he might blunder into a trap. The quick advance into Belgium had stretched out supply lines, and he was concerned about a flank attack. The sound of his panzers echoed from surrounding mountains, and he wondered if he might also be hearing American tanks closing in on him.

Suddenly, looming up out of the fog in front of him, were two civilians walking toward Bastogne. One was unusually tall, and the other was extremely thin. Both wore black berets and appeared to be farmers. They turned around as the panzer column approached. Bayerlein raised his hand, signalling the panzers to stop. He told a few of his aides to come with him and climbed down from the halftrack, heading toward the two men.

"Are you men from around here?" Bayerlein asked with a friendly smile.

"Yes, we're from Bastogne," replied the tall man.

"Are there many Americans there?"

"Oh yes, a great many Americans. And on this road too. When we came by earlier in the day we saw fifty tanks and an American general just a short distance from here."

"*Fifty* tanks, you say?"

"Yes, sir. Just down the road from here."

"About how far would you say?"

"Two or three miles."

"I see. Thank you very much for the information."

The tall man raised his hand. "Heil Hitler."

Bayerlein smiled. "Heil Hitler."

The two men continued their walk and disappeared into the fog. Bayerlein turned to his aides. "You see men," he said, "there are many German sympathizers here in Belgium, thank God."

The officers returned to the halftrack, and now Bayerlein was convinced that the engine sounds he'd heard in the distance belonged to the American armored force directly in front of him. He didn't dare to attack fifty American tanks with his small force, and visibility was too poor to conduct effective battle anyway.

"We'll camp here for the night," he told his aides. "Set up a defensive perimeter and post guards. I also want a patrol sent out to find out exactly where the Americans are."

His orders were passed down, and his tank section prepared to bed down. He didn't know it, but he could have taken Bastogne by surprise that night if he'd pressed on.

BLOODY BASTOGNE

* * *

Ahead of Bayerlein in the fog, Sergeant Mahoney and Private Dunphy walked swiftly toward Bastogne. Dunphy trembled all over, not just from the cold, but from fear.

"Jesus, Sarge," he said, "I still think we should have hid when we heard those tanks coming. What if they shot us?"

"They didn't shoot us," Mahoney replied, "but they probably would have if they'd found us sneaking around in the bushes. We couldn't see what was coming, remember? What if they'd had troops coming on both sides of the road? They would've shot us right on the spot."

"Oh God," Dunphy said, clutching his breast. "I've never been so scared in my life."

"You'll have to get over that," Mahoney told him. "We've still got a long way to Bastogne."

Mahoney and Dunphy continued to trudge through the night and fog. They'd been on the move since early in the day, when they'd left Stembelot. Staying off the roads, they'd cut through woods and fields, moving in a straight line, and thus were able to get in front of the panzer columns advancing on the convoluted road system. When the fog rolled over them, Mahoney had decided to return to the road. Shortly thereafter, they'd encountered Bayerlein's panzers.

Mahoney knew Bastogne was straight ahead and was anxious to get there. He didn't like being in the open in countryside overrun with Germans. In Bastogne he was certain he'd be safe. He was unaware of the massive panzer force bearing down on Bastogne from all directions.

"HALT!" said a voice ahead in the fog.

"Now what?" Mahoney said to Dunphy as they both raised their hands.

Three crouching American soldiers came toward them out of the fog.

"They look like civilians," said one of them.

"But they might be German spies."

Mahoney smiled at them. "We're American soldiers trying to make it back to our lines."

The GIs asked Mahoney and Dunphy what units they were with and became more suspicious by their answers.

"Listen," Mahoney said to them, "we just passed fifteen

German tanks and a bunch of personnel carriers down the road. You'd better let us through so we can tell your C.O."

The GIs searched Mahoney and Dunphy for weapons and upon finding none, marched them back to the American fortifications farther down the road. Soon, through the fog, Mahoney saw houses. They entered a small village where paratroopers from the 101st Airborne were setting up a defense. The guards took them to one of the houses and turned them over to some other soldiers, who locked them in a room.

"Hey—we're American GIs like you!" Mahoney protested.

"Shut the fuck up!" replied a paratrooper, slamming the door in Mahoney's face.

The room had no furniture, so Mahoney and Dunphy sat on the floor.

"What now?" Dunphy asked.

"All we have to do is convince them of who we are," Mahoney replied. "It shouldn't be too hard for you, since you're in the First Army, but I'm not."

Mahoney took out a package of cigarettes and lit one up. He didn't offer one to Dunphy because Dunphy didn't smoke. Mahoney hoped the paratroopers had passed along the word about the German tank force down the road. Surely the Germans would send out a patrol sooner or later to probe for Americans. Mahoney hadn't seen any tanks or tank destroyers in the little village, and it was probable that the paratroopers didn't have them because armor wasn't part of a paratrooper's equipment.

After a while, the door opened, and a corporal pointed to Mahoney. "You—come with me!"

Mahoney got up and followed the corporal out of the room. They crossed a big room where paratroopers were piling furniture in front of the windows and entered another room. A captain smoking a pipe sat behind a shaky field desk. He had crew cut blond hair and the neck of a bull.

"Have a seat," the captain said.

Mahoney sat down, and the captain proceeded to ask questions. Mahoney explained who he was, what he was doing in the Ardennes, and what he'd been through during the past few days, omitting the part about the women on the farm. "There are about fifteen German tanks down the road," Mahoney concluded, "and maybe a hundred German soldiers. I think you'd better get the hell out of here while you've still got the chance."

The captain shook his head. "No," he said, "we're not going anywhere, but you are. I'll have to send you back to Bastogne to get your story checked."

Mahoney felt relieved. "They know me at Eighth Corps headquarters there," he said.

"The Eighth Corps isn't in Bastogne anymore," the captain said. "They've moved to Neufchateau." He pointed to the screaming eagle patch on his arm. "We've got Bastogne now."

TWELVE

Corporal Edward Cranepool of the Hammerhead Division's Fifteenth Regiment sat with other members of his platoon in a bombed out steel mill in the Saar valley, eating C rations and taking a brief respite from the war. They'd just captured the steel mill, and bodies of dead Germans lay near them. Pfc Grossberger, the medic, patched up the GI wounded. The platoon had been ordered to hold the steel mill and await further orders.

Explosions and gunfire could be heard from their left and right, but they ate without showing much concern. Lieutenant Woodward, the new platoon leader, had posted guards, so they wouldn't be taken by surprise.

"Gee," said Pfc Warren Tyler from Biloxi, Mississippi, "I wonder how old Sergeant Mahoney is doing these days."

Cranepool glanced up, because he and Mahoney had been close friends. Cranepool thought of Mahoney as something between a big brother and a father, and wished he'd return to Charlie Company where he belonged.

"Don't worry about Sergeant Mahoney,": replied Pfc

Grossberger, bandaging an arm nearby. "I'm sure he's doing all right."

"Has anybody heard from him?"

Everybody shook his head. Nobody had heard from him.

"You'd think he'd at least write a letter," said Sergeant Leary. "He's probably drunk in some fucking whorehouse someplace, and he's forgotten all about his old platoon."

"Naw," said Cranepool, "he's probably too busy."

"Where in the hell is he supposed to be?" asked Corporal Fanucchi.

Everybody shrugged. Nobody knew exactly where Mahoney was, except that he was somewhere in the First Army on TDY.

Private Antone Sequira looked off into the distance. "I remember the day we went over that river in France—what was that river, Baxter?"

"The Moselle I think it was."

"Yeah, the Moselle. Sergeant Mahoney really was something on that day, bleeding from everyplace but kicking ass everywhere he went. He was killing just about a German every minute."

Private Richardson, a recently arrived replacement who had formerly been a finance clerk, appeared skeptical. "A German a minute! That's impossible!"

Private Sequira grinned. "Not on that day it wasn't. The krauts were as thick as flies. All you had to do was shoot your rifle, and you'd hit one of them."

"Oh-oh," Leary said. "Here comes the looie."

They looked up and saw the new platoon leader, Second Lieutenant Dennis Woodward of Wilmington, Delaware, approaching across the floor of the factory. He was tall and lanky, with the strap from his helmet hanging down to his chest. The men hadn't accepted him yet as one of them because he'd only been around for two weeks, but that didn't seem to bother Woodward at all.

He knelt down among them and chewed gum, looking them over calmly. Sometimes new second lieutenants were intimidated by their men but not Woodward. He'd graduated from West Point six months ago, and it was impossible to intimidate him.

"We've got new orders," he said. "We're going to withdraw from this area during the night and head north. I don't know exactly where we're going yet, but the krauts have launched a big counteroffensive into Belgium, and we've got to go and help out."

"Our whole division?" asked Cranepool.

"This division and two others," Woodward replied, "with the rest of Third Army behind us."

The men lowered their forks and looked at each other in astonishment.

"Holy shit," said Sequira, "that must be a helluva counteroffensive the Germans have got going."

"Must be," replied Woodward. "After you finish chow, get ready to move out."

"I thought you said we wouldn't leave until tonight," Grossberger said.

"It's best to be ready in case we have to go sooner." Woodward stood up. "Carry on." He turned and walked away.

The men of the First Platoon looked at each other.

"This don't sound good," said Sergeant Leary.

Cranepool took out his pack of cigarettes. "Whether we fight the krauts up there or down here—it don't make a fuck to me," he replied.

In Bastogne, General McAuliffe jumped out of his jeep and walked toward the front door of his headquarters building. He wore a zippered battle jacket with a fur collar and his breath made clouds in the cold night air. He was returning from an inspection of fortifications on the edge of the city.

Entering the building, he climbed the stairs and made his way through the long corridors to his office. In the middle of one of the corridors, he heard a deep voice hollering angrily, and McAuliffe thought the string of curses extraordinary. He stopped, turned to the door, and opened it.

He saw a big man wearing civilian clothes sitting on a chair surrounded by paratroopers.

"What the hell's going on in here!" McAuliffe said.

The paratroopers snapped to attention, and so did the man in civilian clothes.

"At ease," General McAuliffe said. He looked at the big man in civilian clothes. "I asked what's going on in here."

"Well, sir," said a first lieutenant, "this man here was picked up by the 501st Parachute regiment and..."

The man in civilian clothes interrupted him. "They didn't pick me up!" he shouted. "I was trying to get back here to Bastogne, and I ran into the stupid bastards!"

McAuliffe looked at him. "Shut up!"

"Yes, sir."

McAuliffe turned to the lieutenant again. "Go on."

"He claims to be from Third Army and he's here on TDY with Eighth Corps, but that sounds fishy to me. He's probably a spy, sir."

"I'm not a spy!" the civilian yelled.

"I thought I told you to shut up," McAuliffe said.

"Sorry sir," said the man, "but I'm getting tired of being treated like a German. I'm an American GI, and I was in Clervaux when the Germans came."

"What were you doing in Clervaux?"

"I was in a whorehouse."

McAuliffe grunted. "He sounds like a real GI to me." He looked at Mahoney carefully and saw the map of Ireland on his face. "What's your name?"

Mahoney told him his name, rank, and serial number, and provided a brief summary of his experiences since Clervaux, leaving out the part about the Belgian women on the farm. McAuliffe knew something about the Hammerhead Division because an old friend of his was one of the regimental commanders. He asked Mahoney a few questions about the Hammerheads, and Mahoney answered all of them satisfactorily.

McAuliffe shrugged. "I think this soldier is who he says he is. Get him a uniform and a rifle, and have him report to my office. He might come in handy for something."

"But sir," protested the lieutenant. "He might have memorized all that information. I think we should lock him up until we know for sure."

"I don't think any German in the world could impersonate a GI from New York this well," he said. "Do as I say."

"Yes, sir."

General McAuliffe left the room and proceeded down the corridor to his office. He entered it and his sharp young paratrooper clerks shot to their feet.

"At ease," he told them, walking to his desk. He took off his helmet and hung up his jacket. His straight black hair was parted almost in the middle, and he smoothed it with his hands as he sat behind his desk.

Lieutenant James, one of his aides, walked through the open door. "Sir?"

McAuliffe looked up. "What is it?"

"General Middleton called, sir. He wanted you to call him as soon as you get back."

"Get him for me."

"Yes, sir."

Lieutenant James picked up the telephone and told the operator to put him through to General Middleton in Neufchateau, while McAuliffe looked over the reports lying on his desk. They indicated that his three combat commands were heavily engaged on the roads leading to Bastogne from the east. He also learned that he didn't have much artillery ammunition left.

Lieutenant James handed him the telephone. "General Middleton will be on directly, sir."

McAuliffe took the phone and held it to his ear as he continued studying the reports. He learned that a new unit, the 705th Tank Destroyer Battalion, had arrived in Bastogne earlier in the afternoon and would stay to help augment the defense of the city.

"Are you there, McAuliffe?" said the voice of General Middleton.

"Yes, sir."

"I'm afraid I've got bad news for you. I found out about an hour ago that you're surrounded."

"Well," McAuliffe said, "that certainly simplifies things, doesn't it?"

"How long do you think you can hold out there?"

"Depends on how many Germans are around me and how badly they want Bastogne."

"We've identified three German divisions and several other smaller German units, and you only have to look on a map to see how badly they want Bastogne."

"Forty-eight hours," McAuliffe said. "After that I can't promise you anything."

"Relief is on the way if you can just hang on. Patton is coming up from the south."

"Patton?" asked McAuliffe. "Maybe things aren't as bad as I thought."

"I don't know how long the wires between your headquarters and mine will remain intact, so good luck to you, McAuliffe, and try to hang on there as best you can."

"We'll have to hang on here, sir," McAuliffe replied. "If we tried to get away now, they'd chew us to pieces."

McAuliffe hung up the phone and stared into the distance for a few moments, trying to come to terms with the fact that he and the 101st Airborne were surrounded in Bastogne.

"Anything serious?" asked Lieutenant James.

"No," replied McAuliffe. "We're just surrounded, that's all."

"Surrounded!"

"That's right. You might as well notify the troops. I guess they should know."

There was a knock on the side of the open door. McAuliffe looked up and saw Mahoney in a new green uniform with a screaming eagle patch on his shoulder.

"Hello there, sir," Mahoney said, strutting into the office. "Here I am reporting for duty, just like you said."

Lieutenant James looked at Mahoney with disapproval and dismay as Mahoney stood in front of General McAuliffe's desk and saluted.

"What do you want me to do, sir?" Mahoney asked.

McAuliffe looked at his watch. "It's chowtime," he said. "Report to me when you come back from the mess hall."

"Yes, sir."

Mahoney did a smart about-face and marched out of the office.

"Who's that?" asked Lieutenant James.

"His name's Mahoney," McAuliffe replied. "He came to Bastogne on TDY and thought he was going to have a little vacation."

"Some vacation."

McAuliffe stood behind his desk. "Let's go to chow," he said.

The enlisted men's mess was in a building down the street, and Mahoney went through the line, holding out his aluminum tray and watching gloomy cooks dump Spam and beans onto it. He poured himself a mug of coffee and then walked toward the tables.

"MAHONEY!" someone cried.

Mahoney looked around and saw the grizzled features of Master Sergeant Frank Hooper coming toward him.

"You old son of a bitch!" Hooper said. "What in the hell are you doing here?"

"The same thing you're doing here."

"Come on and sit down."

Hooper led Mahoney back to the table where he'd been sitting, and Mahoney sat opposite him, slicing a slab of Spam and placing half of it into his mouth.

Hooper looked at Mahoney as if he was seeing a ghost. "What the hell happened to you?" he asked.

Mahoney waved his hand as he chewed the Spam noisily. "You wouldn't believe it."

"How'd you get out of jail?"

"They let us all out and gave us rifles. How did you get here?"

"When I heard the Germans were coming to Clervaux, I got in the first jeep that was coming here. I thought I'd be safe, but now the Germans are getting close, and I want to go south to Third Army. You wanna come with me?"

"You're fucking right I do."

They ate their beans and Spam and hatched a plan to steal a jeep and go south to Third Army, unaware that Bastogne had been surrounded.

Mahoney shoved a spoonful of beans into his mouth and washed it down with hot coffee. "I'm supposed to report to General McAuliffe after chow, but fuck him. I haven't had nothing but trouble since I came to this damned First Army. I want to get back to the Hammerheads *right now.*"

"Me too," replied Hooper.

* * *

After chow, Mahoney and Hooper walked into the 101st Airborne motor pool and approached the desk of the dispatcher. Mahoney and Hooper both wore the screaming eagle patch of the 101st plus regimental insignia and the silver badges awarded to paratroopers after they make five jumps. Actually Mahoney was entitled to wear the badge, since he was once in the Airborne Rangers, but Hooper never had jumped out of an airplane and thought people who did were insane.

"What can I do for you?" asked the dispatcher, a young corporal with the gleam of madness in his eyes common among paratroopers.

"We need a jeep."

The dispatcher looked at their stripes and insignia and said, "Hup, Sarge." He filled out the trip ticket, and Mahoney signed it. Giving Mahoney a copy, he wrote the number of the jeep in the space provided and told Mahoney where to find the vehicle. Mahoney and Hooper walked across the motor pool and got into the jeep. Mahoney turned the switch and started it up.

"This is a nice sounding machine," Mahoney said. "We'll be in Nancy by morning."

Mahoney shifted into gear and drove through the big door into the streets of Bastogne. It was another dark moonless night, and the sounds of fighting could be heard in the distance. The streets were filled with paratroopers and civilians looking for someplace to stay for the night. Mahoney felt guilty about leaving Bastogne, but he felt certain that if he stayed he'd only get into trouble sooner or later with the paratroopers, and they weren't the kind of people that you wanted to mess with. He'd be best off with his own people in the Hammerhead division.

The jeep came to an artillery emplacement in the southern part of town, and a short distance beyond that were some fortifications manned by paratroopers. Mahoney and Hooper waved to them, and they waved back as the jeep passed the fortifications and headed toward the open road. Mahoney shifted into high gear and pressed the accelerator to the floor. The jeep gathered speed and roared down the road to France.

* * *

Throughout Germany, citizens were preparing to go to bed when suddenly on the radio the Victory Fanfare blared forth, and people looked at their loudspeakers in astonishment because there had been no victories reported for almost two years. They all gathered around their radios, whether they lived in opulent mansions or humble farmhouses, and waited anxiously for the music to end so they could hear the news.

Finally the voice of Joseph Goebbels, the Nazi Minister of Propaganda, came to their ears. "People of Germany," he said in a voice laden with urgency and melodrama, "our Fuehrer Adolf Hitler has asked me to tell you that a great victory has been won in the West!" Goebbels paused so that the German people would have some time to recover from that statement, then he continued. "Even as I speak, the armies of the Reich are striking deep into France and Belgium, overwhelming all enemy defenses, and taking thousands of prisoners. This offensive began four days ago in complete secrecy and has taken the Americans by surprise. Only now can the truth be told to you.

"Perhaps you all have been wondering why the Fuehrer has been so silent lately. Perhaps you have thought he was sick. Well, now the truth can be told. The Fuehrer has been in excellent health and has been spending all his time planning this brilliant offensive down to its smallest details. And he has shown his genius once more: the Americans are fleeing before our brave soldiers. Once again, victory is ours!"

Goebbels continued for some time with his speech, and when he finished, a band played "Deutschland Uber Alles." All over Germany, people looked at each other and felt relieved. They'd known they were losing the war, but they'd also believed that somehow they'd recapture the initiative. Now, they realized that their faith had not been in vain. Their leader had transformed defeat into victory, and soon life would be wonderful again as it had been in the great days at the beginning of the war.

The jeep sped through the dark and mysterious night. Mahoney hunched behind the windshield and puffed a cigarette as the windstream whistled over his head. He looked at his watches, and both indicated a few minutes after one o'clock in the morning.

"We should be getting into France pretty soon," Mahoney said.

"Yeah," replied Hooper, glancing at his own collection of watches. "I can't wait to see that old Hammerhead patch again."

"Everything is all fucked up around here," Mahoney said. "These people don't know how to fight a goddamned war. All this shit never would have happened in Third Army."

"You're damned right it wouldn't," Hooper agreed.

Mahoney took the last drag on his cigarette and threw the butt over his shoulder. "Hey," he said, "do you remember that girl I got into a fight over in that bar?"

"You mean the brunette?"

"Yeah—Madeleine."

"She's in Bastogne," Hooper said. "Didn't you know that?"

Mahoney's eyes almost popped out of his head. "In Bastogne?"

"You didn't know that?"

"WHY DIDN'T YOU TELL ME?" Mahoney screamed.

"I didn't think you gave a shit."

Mahoney slammed on the brakes, and the jeep skidded all over the icy, narrow road.

Hooper hung onto his helmet. "What the fuck's the matter with you?"

"WE'RE GOING BACK TO BASTOGNE!" Mahoney yelled as he wrestled with the wheel and struggled to keep the jeep under control.

Finally the jeep stopped. Mahoney shifted into reverse and turned it around while Hooper stared at Mahoney in confusion.

"Are you going psycho on me, Mahoney?" Hooper asked.

"I'm going back to Bastogne."

Mahoney aimed the jeep toward Bastogne and shifted into first, stomping on the gas.

"Hey!" Hooper said. "I don't want to go back to Bastogne!"

"Then jump the fuck out!"

"You're going back to Bastogne just because y⟨ou⟩ see that fucking little whore?"

Mahoney reached to the side with one hand and grab⟨bed⟩ the front of Hooper's field jacket. "What did you call her!"

"Keep your eyes on the road for chrisake!"

"Don't you ever call her that again!"

"Okay—okay!"

Hooper was a brute, but he didn't want to argue with somebody driving a jeep at top speed. If the disagreement had occurred outside the jeep, Hooper would have decked Mahoney or at least tried.

"Where's she at in Bastogne?" Mahoney asked, his foot holding the gas pedal on the floor.

"She's working at the civilian hospital—as a nurse's helper or something like that."

Suddenly the sound of a machine gun ripped the night apart. The windshield of the jeep shattered, and Mahoney already was diving toward the ground. He landed on his left side, bounced, and rolled off into the fresh snow that cushioned him and brought him to a safe stop.

His eyebrows and face covered with snow, he looked up and saw the jeep continuing down the road, disintegrating before his eyes as machine gun bullets tore it apart. He couldn't see whether Hooper was in it or not. The jeep exploded in a fiery red flash, and huge chunks of metal flew into the sky. They fell to earth, burned awhile, and then the night became dark again.

Mahoney lay still, holding his rifle ready. He was bruised all over his body, but he knew somebody had destroyed the jeep and would turn up sooner or later to check on his handiwork. He wondered if Hooper had got out alive.

He heard voices speaking in gutteral German. Three figures emerged out of the darkness and walked cautiously toward the jeep's wreckage. Mahoney took a hand grenade out of the breast pocket of his field jacket. He pulled the pin and waited tensely until the Germans came closer. Slowly, they approached the jeep, and Mahoney could perceive the outlines of their helmets. They stopped beside it and looked into the driver's seat where Mahoney had been thinking about Madeleine only minutes ago.

"Where is he?" asked one of the Germans.

"He must be near here someplace," replied another, turning around.

Mahoney let the hand grenade fly. One of the Germans heard the sound of Mahoney's movement and aimed his rifle in that direction, but Mahoney was already face down in the snow again, and the hand grenade hurtled toward the Germans.

"What's that!" one of them said as it fell near his feet.

The grenade exploded, annihilating the three Germans. Mahoney rose and ran toward them, holding his rifle ready just in case. He saw them sprawled all over the road, gouts of blood everywhere. He was surprised that Germans were south of Bastogne, and these three must be the patrol of a much larger force. He thought he should get back to Bastogne and report this enemy activity to General McAuliffe as soon as possible.

Then his sharp eyes noticed something unusual. The epaulette of one of the Germans had something on it that covered his unit insignia. Mahoney knelt and saw that it was green felt. He tore it away and saw the letters *GD*. Mahoney knew that was the insignia of the famous *Gross Deutschland* Division. He recalled reading somewhere that the crack *Gross Deutschland* Division had been fighting in Russia; what was it doing here in Belgium?

Mahoney thought he'd better relay this information to General McAuliffe, but first he wanted to check on Hooper. He made his way back to the spot where the jeep had been when the firing began. A figure lay in the snow beside the road. Mahoney knelt beside it. Hooper lay on his back, with his eyes wide open and staring and blood freezing on the front of his field jacket. Mahoney felt for a pulse, but there was nothing at all. Opening Hooper's field jacket, he grabbed Hooper's dog tags and tore them away, dropping them into his pocket.

"So long, old buddy," he said to Hooper's corpse.

Turning, he walked back to Bastogne.

In a small village in eastern Belgium, Field Marshal Model was sound asleep in his new headquarters, which had formerly been a schoolhouse. There was a knock on the do[or] he stirred.

"Who's there?" he called out sleepily.

The door opened. "The Fuehrer wishes to speak with you immediately!" said an aide silhouetted by the light in the corridor behind him.

Model stuck his monocle in his eye and looked at his watch. It was three o'clock in the morning. Grumbling, he rolled out of bed and put his greatcoat over his pajamas and his hat on his head because he sometimes got chills through his bald spot. Stepping into his boots, he left his bedroom and walked down the hall to the conference room, where he'd take the call. He knew that the Fuehrer must be displeased about something and prepared himself for the worst.

"This is Field Marshal Model," he said into the telephone.

"Why have you not taken Bastogne?" Hitler asked, anger and condemnation in his voice.

"We've only reached Bastogne yesterday, my Fuehrer. The Americans are fighting with unusual tenacity. Bastogne should fall into our hands today."

"Model," Hitler said, "as I look at my maps I see Bastogne as the main impediment to our progress. It has become the most important objective in our entire offensive. Do not fail me, Model. We must have Bastogne today."

"Yes, sir."

After hanging up, Model called General Hasso von Manteuffel and relayed the message from Hitler. Manteuffel then relayed it to General Bayerlein of the Panzer Lehr Division and the other divisional commanders surrounding Bastogne.

It was clearly understood that Bastogne would have to be taken that day, the 21st of December.

THIRTEEN

At ten o'clock in the morning, the Third Army was rumbling north on a twenty mile front. The men of the Hammerhead Division rode on tanks, and when they reached Luxembourg City, the citizens came out into the streets to cheer because they'd expected the Germans to attack at any moment, but instead the Americans had arrived to protect them.

"PATTON—PATTON—PATTON!" the people chanted, waving American flags and throwing flowers at the soldiers.

Cranepool and his squad rode on one of the lead tanks, and he caught a wreath with the end of his rifle. There was pandemonium everywhere he looked. Girls blew kisses at him, and he wished he could climb down from the tank and grab a few of them. A bottle came flying through the air, and Pfc Grossberger caught it like Joe Dimaggio playing center field. It was red wine, and he dug out the cork with the blade of his penknife.

"PATTON—PATTON—PATTON!" the people screamed.

Slowly the men and tanks made their way through the jubilation, drinking wine and ogling the girls. A massive traffic jam caused the tanks to stop, and little children climbed all over the soldiers, begging for chocolate and touching their uniforms. A few girls made it onto the tanks, and officers loudly instructed the men to leave them alone, but the officers couldn't see everything, and a few kisses were stolen, not to mention some cheap feels.

Finally the armored column moved out again. It rumbled through the cheering throngs, and Cranepool thought he and the other soldiers might as well enjoy themselves while they could, because soon they'd be in Belgium fighting the biggest German counteroffensive of the war.

Cranepool's tank approached an intersection, and he saw a

soldier directing traffic. Men on the lead tanks were pointing to the soldier, and Cranepool leaned forward so he could get a better look. MPs held back the crowds, who applauded and shouted in a mad frenzy.

"IT'S OLD BLOOD AND GUTS!" somebody yelled.

Cranepool saw the stars on the soldier's epaulettes, and stared in amazement at General George S. Patton Jr. waving the tanks through.

He'd been the one who unsnarled the traffic jam.

Mahoney spent the night trudging through the woods, because he was afraid to use the road now that Germans were in the vicinity. He was angry with himself for leaving Bastogne although he kept telling himself that he had no way of knowing that Germans were to the south of the city. It had seemed a good idea at the time, but like many good ideas, it had turned to shit.

In the dawn, he saw a huge open space ahead of him through the trees and moved toward it cautiously, thinking it was an open field. Instead, it turned out to be a river valley. The water looked deep and fast, and Mahoney didn't feel like swimming through it in subfreezing weather. He no longer had binoculars, but he knew the general direction of the road and thought he might be able to dash across the bridge if no Germans were around.

He moved through the woods, and after half an hour he spotted a Bailey bridge over the river. Making his way closer to it, he stopped abruptly when he saw soldiers crawling all over it. He didn't know whether they were American or German, but assumed they were Americans and were preparing to blow the bridge. Creeping closer, he recognized American uniforms and knew he was safe at last.

He came out of the woods and walked toward the soldiers, slinging his rifle over his shoulder. Some of the soldiers ran toward him and challenged him. He gave them the password he'd learned last night in Bastogne, and they permitted him to continue.

He walked onto the bridge and saw soldiers setting TNT charges. A lieutenant was on the far side with some sergeants and a map, and Mahoney walked toward him.

"Sir," Mahoney said, "I ran into a German patrol on that road last night, and I think it might be a good idea to blow this bridge in a hurry, before they move their main forces into this area."

The lieutenant looked at Mahoney suspiciously. Like everyone else on the bridge, he wore the screaming eagle patch on his shoulder. "Who the hell are you?" he asked.

Mahoney explained who he was and said he'd been out on patrol when he'd encountered the Germans. He neglected to mention that he was trying to escape to the Third Army in the south.

"Do you know anything about explosives?" the lieutenant asked.

"Yes, sir."

"Then you just volunteered to help out here."

Mahoney leaned his rifle against a stack of paratrooper rifles and walked back to the bridge. He saw that the work was only about a quarter done, and pitched in to help, tying packets of TNT to the bridge and running the wires back to where the lieutenant stood with the detonator.

Some paratroopers ran toward the bridge from the south. "Sir," one of them yelled, "the Germans are coming!"

"How many?" the officer called back.

"An armored column—maybe twenty tanks or more—and some personnel carriers!"

The lieutenant ran onto the bridge. "Let's go men—we don't have much time!"

Fortunately most of the charges were in place. Mahoney took some of the blasting caps and wire and ran to the far side of the bridge, where he inserted the caps into the bundles of TNT and then hooked up the wires. He worked his way backwards, crawling over the bridge's girders like a big monkey, while the paratroopers performed the same function on the other side of the bridge.

Finally, all the caps were set and the wires connected. They ran the wires back to the magneto and tied them in while in the distance they could hear the rumble of the advancing German convoy.

"Thank God, we did it in time," the lieutenant said, chewing his lower lip. "Let's get ready to pull the hell out of here."

Mahoney tied the last wire to the terminal post of the magneto, then stood. "Sir," he said, "why don't we wait until the German tanks are on the bridge? Then we can destroy a few of them along with it."

The lieutenant had a big jowly face. "Too risky," he said. "I want to blow the bridge and get my men the hell back to Bastogne."

"All you need are a couple of men here, sir. The rest can return to Bastogne."

"Are you volunteering, Sergeant?"

"Why not? Are you?"

The officer turned red because he didn't expect Mahoney to turn it around on him. He was in a corner, and all he could say was "Sure."

The officer told one of his sergeants to take the rest of the men back to Bastogne, and he and Mahoney would catch up with them later on the road. The sergeant lined up the men and told them to load into the deuce and a half truck that had brought them to the bridge. A jeep was left behind for Mahoney, the lieutenant, whose name was Zowski, and Zowski's driver, Pfc Manuel Arruda from Gloucester, Mass. The deuce and a half sped away.

Mahoney, Zowski, and Arruda moved into some trees nearby, taking the detonator and a box containing four bunches of TNT sticks that hadn't been used. Just as they were getting into position, the German armored column came around the bend three hundred yards away and thundered toward the bridge, its tracks kicking up clods of ice and snow.

"Here they come," said Zowski, peering at them through his binoculars.

Mahoney clutched the detonator in his left hand and its handle in his right. He could make out the figures of the tank commanders standing in the turrets of their white tanks. They approached the bridge, and Mahoney held the detonator more tightly.

"Get ready," said Zowski.

The first tank rolled onto the bridge, followed by the second and then the third. The entire bridge could only hold four tanks at a time, and as soon as the fourth one was aboard, Zowski shouted, "NOW!"

Mahoney twisted the handle.

And nothing happened.

Mahoney twisted it again, and still the bridge didn't blow. The first tank rolled off the bridge to the near side.

"WHAT THE HELL'S THE PROBLEM!" Zowski screamed.

Mahoney twisted the handle again, but still the TNT didn't go off. Sweat appeared on his forehead although the temperature was twenty-eight degrees. A second tank rolled off the near side of the bridge.

Mahoney uttered a prayer and twisted again. The wires crackled with electricity, and there was an earsplitting explosion as the bridge disappeared in a huge cloud of smoke. The fierce wind blew the smoke away quickly, revealing no more bridge. The tanks that had been on it had fallen into the river below, and the water was so deep they couldn't be seen.

The commander of the second tank that made it across the bridge had been hit in the back by a chunk of shrapnel and lay dead or wounded in his turret. His crew pulled him into the tank and closed the hatch. The commander of the first tank had already disappeared, and his turret was moving to the side, trying to get a view of what had happened.

Mahoney pulled a bunch of TNT sticks from the box and lit the fuse with a match.

"What the hell are you going to do!" screamed Zowski, looking at the burning fuse with horror.

"We gotta get those tanks before they get us!"

Mahoney stuffed another bunch of TNT sticks into his field jacket pocket, then leapt up and ran toward the lead tank, the TNT with the burning fuse in his hand and his arm cocked back. Somebody in the first tank must have seen him because the cannon and turret swung suddenly in his direction.

Mahoney hurled the TNT high into the air and dove into the snow. The TNT with its burning fuse fell onto the turret of the tank, rolled to its front deck, and dropped onto the ground. Mahoney took the second bunch of TNT out of his pocket and lit the fuse. It sizzled, and he gritted his teeth as he pulled his arm and prepared to throw it.

Just then the first bunch of TNT exploded. It had been on the ground in front of the first tank, and it blew the tank 15 feet into the air, ripping apart its hull and incinerating everybody inside. Mahoney ducked, then lit the second fuse and threw the TNT at the other tank.

As soon as the TNT left his hand, machine gun bullets kicked up snow in front of him. He kept his head low and wished a brick wall was in front of him. The second bunch of TNT sticks landed a few yards from the tank that was firing its two machine guns at Mahoney. The turret of the tank opened suddenly, and one of the crew members pulled himself out. Mahoney realized the German was trying to throw the TNT away before it exploded.

A single shot was fired from the direction of the woods, and the tanker froze for a few seconds, then sagged to the side. The TNT exploded and once again the valley was filled with thunder and smoke as the tank's side was split open and broken apart.

Mahoney was on his feet and running before all the debris had hit the ground. German tanks on the far side of the river fired their machine guns at him, and the bullets sounded like angry gnats around his ears. He dived into the bushes and landed a few feet from Zowski.

"LET'S GET THE FUCK OUT OF HERE!" Mahoney yelled.

Mahoney picked up his rifle, and they all ran to the jeep. Pfc Arruda started the engine, and the jeep spun its wheels on the snow, then bolted out of the woods and headed for the road. German machine gun bullets cracked over their heads, and an artillery shell from a tank landed a hundred yards away.

"GO!" yelled Mahoney, holding his helmet onto his head.

Arruda turned left when he reached the road and stomped the accelerator onto the floor. A curve in the road was fifty yards in front of them, and if they could get around it, they'd be safe. The German tankers fired more shells and machine gun bullets, but the little jeep was too fast for them, and it scooted behind the hill.

Mahoney took a deep breath. "We made it," he sighed, as the jeep careened down the road to Bastogne.

Zowski slapped Mahoney on the shoulder. "You're a helluva guy!" he said. "I'll have to put you in for a medal when we get back."

"I'd settle for a good cigar. You wouldn't happen to have one on you by any chance, would you?"

"Wouldn't I?" Zowski unzipped his field jacket, reached

inside, and produced three cigars. He passed them out, lit them with his lighter, and they all puffed happily as they sped toward Bastogne.

General Bradley entered General Eisenhower's office at Versailles. Ike looked up from the map table, his eyes bleary from insufficient sleep. Bradley saluted and approached the map table.

"You wanted to see me, sir?"

Ike nodded. "I'm afraid I have bad news for you, Brad. The German advance is continuing unabated, and it seems to me that you're getting cut off from your two armies in the north. Therefore, I've decided to appoint General Montgomery as temporary commander of those troops until this mess is cleared up."

Bradley looked at the map and swallowed. "But you're taking away half of my command, sir."

"It has to be done, Brad. I don't see how you can command them effectively from here. It's no reflection on your abilities." Ike pointed to the map. "It's just that we've got this goddamned German bulge in our territory, and we've got to get rid of it in the best way that we can."

Bradley felt a flare of anger and thought he ought to resign on the spot, but realized he was only a soldier and had to obey orders just like everybody else.

"Yes, sir," he said in as strong a voice as he could muster.

Nobody at General McAuliffe's headquarters knew who Mahoney was, so he had to bully and bluff his way upstairs to the conference room where McAuliffe was having a meeting with his top commanders and aides.

They discussed the immediate formation of a special combat team consisting of eight tanks that could be rushed quickly to any threatened sector of the city. Then they thought they should organize a few more mobile emergency teams in case the Germans attacked at more than one point at the same time.

McAuliffe happened to look up and found himself looking

at Mahoney. At first he didn't know who he was but then remembered.

"Where the hell have you been?" McAuliffe asked.

"Well," replied Mahoney, "I took a little patrol south to see what was there, and this is what I found." He tossed the German epaulette in front of McAuliffe, who picked it up and examined it in the light.

"This looks like the unit designation of the *Gross Deutschland* Division," McAuliffe said. "Last thing I heard, they were fighting in Russia."

Mahoney nodded. "We're fighting units that aren't even supposed to be here."

McAuliffe passed the epaulette to his G-2 officer. "Pass this information along to Corps if you can get through."

"Yes, sir."

McAuliffe was about to congratulate Mahoney when there was a knock on the door.

"Come in!" said McAuliffe.

A captain entered the conference room and saluted. "Sir, we've got four German officers outside who're carrying a truce flag. They've brought a note for you from their commander."

The captain handed the note to McAuliffe, who read it quickly.

"Nuts," he said, throwing the note onto the table.

"What did it say, sir?" asked one of the aides.

"It says that they've got us surrounded, and they're offering us the opportunity to surrender." McAuliffe looked at the captain. "Escort them back to wherever they came from."

"They said they need a written reply, sir."

"I don't care what they need."

"Sir," said the captain, "they've delivered a bona fide military communication, and I think that under the commonly observed rules of war they're entitled to a written answer."

McAuliffe looked annoyed. "Well, what should I tell them?"

"Tell them to go fuck themselves," Mahoney said.

"That's no good," said an aide.

"What about your first remark?" asked the captain.

"What remark was that?" said McAuliffe.

"Nuts."

McAuliffe shrugged and bent over the map table. He picked up a pencil, wrote *nuts* at the bottom of the surrender request, and signed his name.

"Here you go," he said to the captain, handing him the piece of paper.

After the meeting, Mahoney slipped out of the headquarters building and set off in search of Madeleine. He stopped a civilian in the street, asked him where the civilian hospital was, and received directions.

Mahoney made his way across battle torn Bastogne. Enemy artillery bombardments and air attacks had destroyed numerous buildings, transforming them into flat, empty lots. Other buildings had only a wall or two standing. Paratroopers double-timed through the streets, moving from one trouble spot to another, and the air was filled with the sounds of artillery explosions and small arms fire. Many buildings and piles of rubble were burning, and the stench was terrible. Mahoney thought Bastogne was the closest thing to hell he'd ever seen.

Finally he came to the hospital, and some of its walls had been damaged by shell bursts. He went inside and stepped over civilians lying in the reception area and the corridors. The air was heavy with the smell of chemicals and rotting flesh. Nobody stopped him, so he walked down a corridor and into a ward, where beds were crammed together and wounded people moaned pathetically.

"May I help you?" asked an elderly nurse.

"I'm looking for a civilian woman who's working here," Mahoney replied. "Her name is Madeleine."

"Madeleine what?"

"I'm afraid I don't know."

"I don't know anyone named Madeleine," the nurse said. "Perhaps you should check with the main office."

"Where's that?"

The nurse told him how to get to the office, and Mahoney headed in that direction, elated to think he was getting closer to Madeleine. He admitted to himself that she'd probably forgotten him by now because she met so many men, but something made him believe that she remembered him and would be happy to see him again.

He found the office and asked Madeleine's whereabouts. An elderly male clerk told him the number of the ward she worked in, and he said her last name was Devereaux.

Lizards crawled through Mahoney's stomach as he hurried to the ward where she worked. He worried that maybe Madeleine Devereaux wasn't the Madeleine that he was looking for, but he clicked his teeth together and stepped swiftly as he moved along.

The ward was filled with injured children, and they looked at Mahoney with big, sad eyes that asked, *Why is this happening to us*? Mahoney became overwhelmed by melancholy as he gazed at them. He had accepted the war as a fact of his life, and it had become almost ordinary to him, but now, in a room full of injured children, old, forgotten attitudes emerged though the layers of personality, and he realized that war was beastly and unnatural, and that it accomplished nothing except the widespread dissemination of misery.

Mahoney noticed a chubby woman with enormous breasts who was arranging the covers on a little boy. She wore a civilian dress, and Mahoney walked toward her. She looked up as he approached.

"Yes?" she said.

"I'm looking for Madeleine Devereaux," Mahoney said.

"She's sleeping right now."

"Can you tell me where she is?"

"She's sleeping in the basement, but you shouldn't disturb her because she was up for over twenty-four hours straight before she went to bed. She needs to rest."

"Yes, of course," Mahoney said, embarrassed that he'd come to the hospital to make love to a woman who was pushing herself to the limits of human endurance taking care of little children. "But just tell me something, so that I'll know if she's the Madeleine I'm looking for. Is she about this big," Mahoney held out the palm of his hand at her height, "with brown hair, brown eyes, and very pretty?"

The woman smiled. "That's her. Would you like me to give her a message for you?"

"Yes, if you would."

Mahoney racked his brain for an appropriate message, but everything he thought of seemed corny and ridiculous.

"Never mind," Mahoney said. "I'll come back some other time."

"Shall I tell her your name?"

"Mahoney," he replied.

He turned to walk away, and saw two big eyes staring at him. They stopped him cold.

"Can this kid eat candy?" Mahoney asked.

"Yes, he can."

Mahoney reached into his pocket and took out a Hershey bar. Breaking it in half, he gave one piece to the child in front of him and the other piece to the child in the next bed. The woman watched benevolently, as the children solemnly put the chocolate into their mouths and took bites. Then, as the taste of fine American chocolate rolled over their tongues, they smiled happily. The other children rustled in their beds and held out their hands, grinning with expectation.

But Mahoney had nothing to give them. "Sorry kids," he said, "that's all I've got."

The kids continued to hold out their hands, their eyes pleading for candy. Mahoney wished he had a whole truckful of the stuff to give them. He looked at the woman, who nodded in understanding.

"The poor children," she said. "And Christmas is coming, too."

Mahoney blinked because he's lost track of dates and time. "When's Christmas?" he asked.

"Only four days," she told him.

Mahoney left the hospital, wondering how he could steal some candy for the kids. He knew that every box of C rations contained a candy bar, so he thought he'd find out where the C rations were kept and have a little talk with the quartermaster. There were only about forty kids in the ward. It shouldn't be too difficult to steal forty candy bars.

He stepped onto the sidewalk, and darkness already had fallen on Bastogne. Two columns of paratroopers double-timed by, and a lieutenant as tall as Mahoney pointed at him and shouted, "Hey soldier—what are you doing here?"

"Just visiting somebody," Mahoney replied.

"Fall in at the end of this column!"

"Yes, sir."

Mahoney unslung his M-1 and held it at port arms. When the end of the column came abreast of him, he ran into the street and joined the paratroopers. He could have protested and said he was part of General McAuliffe's personal staff, but he knew that Bastogne was surrounded and thought he should do whatever he was asked.

He double-timed with the paratroopers through the streets of Bastogne. Shells exploded in the sky, casting eerie flashing lights on devastated buildings. Machine gun fire could be heard from points all over the city, and the ground heaved with the impact of explosions.

Mahoney's ears picked out the sound of a shell whistling down on him.

"HIT IT!" the lieutenant screamed.

The paratroopers fled in all directions, diving into alleys, storefronts, and through windows. Mahoney landed in a cellar as the shell slammed into the street and exploded with a mighty roar, throwing cobblestones and huge chunks of frozen earth into the air.

The lieutenant blew his whistle, and the paratroopers reformed their column of ducks in the street. They double-timed again, holding their rifles at high port arms. They were a snappy bunch of tough, disciplined soldiers because paratroopers were a special elite in the Army and all of them were volunteers who wanted to be more than ordinary dogfaces.

Mahoney felt good to be among them because he'd been in an elite unit once, the Twenty-third Rangers, and they'd been efficient, professional soldiers who knew their way around a battlefield, unlike the draftees and eight balls who filled the ranks of line divisions like the Hammerheads. Mahoney had transferred out of the Rangers because he'd thought they got too many suicide assignments, but sometimes he thought he'd made a mistake, because the Hammerheads drew their share of difficult assignments too, and although the Hammerhead Division was a good outfit, it was nowhere near as sharp or as professional as a ranger or paratrooper unit.

Mahoney's ears told him they were headed toward a scene of fierce fighting. The Germans must be trying to break through someplace. They turned a corner, and Mahoney saw a six foot barricade of bricks and rubble ahead. Paratroopers lay all over it, firing rifles and anti-tank weapons. American tanks and tank destroyers sat behind it, shooting their cannons and machine guns.

"HALT!" shouted the lieutenant.

Mahoney and the other paratroopers stopped.

"FALL OUT AND TAKE POSITIONS OVER THERE!"

The paratroopers broke ranks and ran toward the barricade. Nobody had to tell them not to bunch up or how to position themselves. They were crackerjack soldiers, and eagerly they climbed the barricade. Mahoney found a spot for himself and looked over the top.

He saw twenty German tanks and about a hundred German soldiers advancing across an icy plain toward the barricade. Between this attacking force and the barricade were destroyed German tanks and corpses, which meant that the Germans had tried to storm the barricade before without success.

A German tank fired its cannon, and a length of the barricade not far from Mahoney was blown apart along with the paratroopers who'd been on top of it. Seconds later, an American anti-tank gun fired, and the tank seemed to shrink as it disappeared in an explosion and cloud of smoke.

Another tank fired at the barricade, scoring a direct hit, but it wasn't enough to blow a path through it, and that's what the Germans wanted to do. American anti-tank guns kept them back, and the German soldiers huddled behind their tanks. Mahoney looked through his sights for a German to shoot but couldn't get a clear shot at any of them. He squeezed off a few rounds anyway, to make them keep their heads down.

The battlefield flashed with light as shells exploded and then went dark while the gunners loaded up again. American and German shells flew back and forth intermittently. Evidently, the Germans were getting ready to attack again. Then, out of the night came a swarm of German tanks, including some of the new Tiger Kings, to augment the German tank force already there. They all joined together and charged the barricade.

Mahoney fired his rifle at the onrushing tanks, although he knew his bullets would do no good. The tanks were such a formidable force that Mahoney figured they'd have to break through. American anti-tank gunners managed to knock out a few of the tanks, but the rest of them kept charging, their engines roaring. They fired their cannons at the barricades, and suddenly Mahoney felt the whole world exploding around him. His ears filled with thunder, and he felt himself falling backward as if he was made of paper.

He didn't know how long he was unconscious, but when he opened his eyes he was in a crouch, half-covered with rubble. Looking around, he saw that twenty tanks had broken through the barricade and were loose in the outskirts of Bastogne. American anti-tank gunners tried to pick them off, but the tanks were at close range, and their machine guns ripped up the Americans.

Mahoney twisted and kicked, trying to get loose from the rubble. He worked himself free and stepped away from the mess, with bruises all over his body. His helmet felt strange, and when he touched it, he found a big dent over his forehead.

He heard shouting and turned to see German foot soldiers pouring through the holes the tanks had blasted through the barricades.

"FIX BAYONETS!" somebody shouted.

Mahoney pulled his bayonet and stuck it on the end of his rifle. He and the paratroopers in the vicinity ran toward the Germans to prevent them from penetrating too deeply into the city. The American paratroopers and German soldiers closed with each other and fought hand to hand. Mahoney stabbed wildly with his bayonet and slammed Germans with his rifle butt, thinking of the children in the hospital and how these Germans must be kept away from them. When he could get a clear shot, he fired his rifle at the Germans, and when the press of fighting became too tight, he used his knees and elbows.

Bayonets slashed his sleeves and the front of his jacket. German submachine gun bullets whizzed around him, and one grazed his helmet, leaving another dent. A German officer aimed a pistol at Mahoney's nose, but Mahoney dove toward the German's ankles as the bullet zipped over his head. He tackled the German officer, brought him down, and then jumped on him, grabbing him by the neck and squeezing.

The German officer gripped Mahoney's wrists and tried to

push him away, but Mahoney was too strong. The officer's eyes bulged, and his tongue stuck out of his mouth. Mahoney squeezed with all his might and felt something go *snap* in his hands.

A German clobbered Mahoney over the head with his rifle butt, and Mahoney toppled to the side. He rolled onto his back and blinked his eyes, trying to make the cobwebs go away. A gleaming German bayonet streaked toward his stomach, and Mahoney batted it out of the way with his forearm. The steel of the bayonet struck the pavement beside Mahoney and threw off sparks. Mahoney leapt up and grabbed the German's rifle. The German tried to kick Mahoney away, and his boot whacked against Mahoney's ribs, but it wasn't enough of a blow to knock Mahoney out of the ballgame. Mahoney brought his own boot up and kicked the German hard between his legs. The German howled and let go his rifle, clutching his balls with both hands. Mahoney, enraged by the sneak attack this German had launched against him, took the rifle and rammed the butt into the German's face.

When Mahoney pulled the rifle back, the German's nose was flattened and his lips were split open. He went slack and dropped to the ground, but Mahoney cracked him once more before he landed.

Around Mahoney men were grunting and shouting, looking into each other's blazing eyes and trying to rip out each other's guts. Mahoney turned the German soldier's rifle around so that he could use the bayonet and attacked the nearest German, a private who didn't look much more than sixteen years old. The young soldier saw Mahoney coming, but he didn't flinch or try to run away. Instead he stood his ground and tried to parry the thrust of Mahoney's bayonet, but he didn't have the strength. His parry only deflected Mahoney's bayonet an inch or two to the side, and instead of receiving the bayonet in his heart, he got it right in the middle of his chest.

The bayonet went in to the hilt, and Mahoney couldn't yank it out. He pulled the trigger of the rifle, but nothing happened. The young German must have emptied a clip and hadn't had time to reload. Mahoney looked frantically on the ground for something to fight with and spotted a German submachine gun, his favorite weapon for close fighting.

He bent over to pick it up, but a German soldier appeared from the crowd of squirming, struggling soldiers around Mahoney and tried to harpoon Mahoney with his bayonet. Mahoney saw the metallic gleam just in time and pulled back. The bayonet streaked past his chest, and he grabbed the German's rifle, wrenching it out of his hands and hitting him in the shoulder with a horizontal butt stroke.

The German lost his balance and stepped backwards. Mahoney went after him and slashed down with the bayonet, which hit the German in the face, sliced through his cheek, cut off his tongue, ripped apart his jaw muscles, and came out through his other cheek.

The German raised his hands and tried to hold his face together, as blood streamed through his fingers. Mahoney pulled his rifle back and then shot it forward, sinking the bayonet into the German's stomach, then yanking it out easily as the German collapsed onto the sidewalk.

Mahoney looked around for the submachine gun. Another German soldier ran toward him, and Mahoney threw the German rifle at him, making him swerve out of the way. Mahoney scooped the submachine gun up from the ground, spread his legs apart, bent his knees, and fired at the German. The burst of bullets shattered the German's ribs and lungs, and the German went flying backwards.

Mahoney held the submachine gun tightly because in close fighting you didn't want to hit any of your own people. He fired it carefully, blowing away one German after another. The submachine gun shook in his hands, and he loved the feel of it and the way it demolished any German who stood in front of him.

Mahoney heard a series of ferocious explosions behind him. Glancing backwards, he saw one of the King Tigers and two other German tanks shattered and belching smoke. Then, before his eyes, another of the German tanks blew apart in a brilliant red flash.

Mahoney shouted victoriously. One of General McAuliffe's mobile tank units finally had arrived at the trouble spot. He charged the Germans in front of him, tearing apart their faces and torsos with bursts of submachine gun fire, and they fell back because they could see their tanks retreating.

The two groups of soldiers separated, as the Germans

retreated and the Americans tried to get out of their way. Mahoney looked around, saw that no tank was about to run him over, and dropped to one knee, firing the submachine gun at the fleeing Germans. He cut a few of them down, and then the submachine gun ran out of ammo. Looking around, he couldn't see any other submachine guns, so he picked up an M-1 lying next to a dead American paratrooper.

He heard a terrific roar behind him and turned to see a German tank bearing down on him. He ran to the side, but another German tank was heading in that direction too. Everywhere he looked, he saw German tanks coming at him, and some of them were the monstrous King Tigers. They fired their cannons at the force of American tanks and tank destroyers pursuing them and rumbled angrily toward safety.

Mahoney didn't know which way to run because German tanks were everywhere. He dodged one of them, and it passed by, spewing out a cloud of diesel smoke that made Mahoney cough. He ran by another tank, and then, twenty yards in front of him, one of the big King Tiger tanks was hit in the treads by an anti-tank shell.

Mahoney pulled a hand grenade out of his pocket because he knew what was coming next. Sure enough, the hatch on top of the tank opened, and a head appeared, because the tankers inside wanted to get out of the big, stationary target. Mahoney ran toward the tank, jumped onto its rear deck, and the German tanker turned around. Mahoney punched him in the mouth, threw the grenade down the hatch, and jumped off the tank, running as fast as he could toward safety.

His grenade exploded inside the Tiger King, and a column of smoke shot straight into the air from the turret. Mahoney stopped to let another German tank pass, and when it came abreast of him, he tossed a grenade into its treads, then ran in a crouch behind the tank.

That grenade ripped the tank's treads apart, so it couldn't move anymore. Mahoney paused on the other side of the tank, took out a third grenade, and pulled the pin. As soon as the tank's hatch opened, he lobbed the grenade inside and then resumed his dash for safety.

He dashed over the cobblestones and couldn't throw more hand grenades at tanks because he didn't have any left. Tanks roared by him like angry elephants, and he tried his best to stay below their machine gun fire, but despite his efforts, a few of the big bullets whizzed past him, and he almost could feel their heat against his face.

Finally, he ran clear of the retreating tanks and climbed up on a barricade, where he saw an anti-tank gun that had fallen onto its side, with dead paratroopers lying around it, evidently the victims of an exploding shell.

Fortunately, the shell hadn't blown up the anti-tank ammunition. Mahoney fed a round into the back, closed the backplate, and took aim at one of the German tanks. He pulled the trigger, and the tank's turret was blown away in a sudden blinding flash. Loading the anti-tank gun again, he fired at a big retreating Tiger King, but he'd aimed too quickly, and the shell flew over the tank, exploding harmlessly onto the ground.

The German tanks retreated until they were out of sight in the darkness. Paratroopers in the street and on the barricade cheered, and Mahoney took out a cigarette and lit it up. He felt exhausted, and his uniform was torn to shreds.

The crews of the American tanks and tank destroyers opened up their hatches and came into the cold night air to cheer along with the paratroopers. The mobile defense force had stopped the Germans this time, but what would they do if the Germans attacked in force at three or four points in the city at once?

Mahoney decided he didn't want to think about that just then. He sat down on the barricade and puffed his cigarette, hoping help would arrive before things got worse in Bastogne.

The Hammerhead Division stopped for the night near the town of Arlon in southern Belgium. General Barton Hughes, the divisional commander, sat inside his command post tent, poring over maps and trying to determine the best routes for his regiments to take tomorrow.

His tent flap opened, and one of his clerks entered. "Sir, Colonel Simmons would like to see you."

"Send him right in."

The clerk departed, and several seconds later, Colonel

Simmons entered the small, enclosed space. He walked to Hughes's desk and saluted, and Hughes pointed to a chair. "Have a seat."

Simmons was a tall officer with graying hair and a pot belly. He sat and looked at General Hughes, who was still poring over papers on his desk. Hughes puffed a pipe, and his face was covered with acne scars partially hidden by a big black mustache. He'd only commanded the Hammerhead Division for six weeks, taking over when the previous C.O. had been killed in action trying to lead some men up a hill. Simmons didn't know what to make of Hughes, who could be a real hard ass at times, but who seemed to know what he was doing usually.

Finally Hughes looked up. "What's the problem?" he said abruptly.

Simmons couldn't help missing old General Donovan, who had usually greeted him with a smile and some bourbon whisky, but for Hughes he sat erectly and said, "Sir, some of the men in my regiment have asked me to speak with you. It seems that a sergeant from Charlie Company is in Bastogne right now on TDY, or at least they think he'd there right now, and they'd like you to send our regiment into Bastogne first, so they can get him out."

Hughes shrugged. "He might not be there anymore."

"The men know that, sir, but they want to get in there first anyway. They all think he's still alive. I know him pretty well, and he's one of those guys who always comes out of the horseshit smelling like a rose."

Hughes was surprised that such a fuss was being made over one soldier. "What's his name?"

"Master Sergeant C. J. Mahoney, sir."

Hughes scratched his head. "Seems to me that name rings a bell."

"He's the divisional heavyweight champion, sir."

"Oh yes, of course," Hughes said. "Now I remember who he is. Wasn't he one of our first men to enter Saarlautern?"

"That's the one, sir."

Hughes recalled meeting Mahoney briefly. He'd been a big mean looking son of a bitch. Hughes figured that if some of the men in the Fifteenth Regiment were anxious to rescue

Mahoney, they might fight a little harder on the way to Bastogne.

"All right," Hughes said. "The Fifteenth goes first. I imagine you might want to put Mahoney's company right up on the point."

"Yes sir—that had been my intention."

"Good. Go to it, Simmons. Anything else?"

"No, sir."

"We expect to make contact with the Germans sometime tomorrow," Hughes said. "I want you to hit them hard and not stop for anything."

"You don't have to worry about my men hitting the Germans hard," Colonel Simmons replied. "They'll be going for broke all the way to Bastogne."

FOURTEEN

Early in the morning, Field Marshal Bernard Law Montgomery strolled into the new office of General Courtney Hodges in Chaudfontaine. Montgomery wore a waist-length battle jacket and a red paratrooper beret at a jaunty angle. He was a slender sparrow of a man and was accompanied by several of his top aides, many of whom had been with him since Africa.

Monty rubbed his hands together as he approached Hodges at the map table. "Well," he said, "we seem to have got ourselves into a difficult situation down here, haven't we? What are the latest dispositions?"

Hodges, dignified and calm as always, pointed to the map and explained the deployment of his men. He told Montgomery that he thought the German attack had slowed considerably and that the time had come to counterattack.

"Oh no, no," Monty said, shaking his head. "We can't do that yet. First, we must tidy up our lines."

"Tidy our lines?" Hodges asked.

"Yes." Monty pointed to the positions of the American Eighty-second Airborne Division, which had already attacked the Germans near St. Vith and gained considerable ground. "You'll have to pull back these units here so that we can straighten out our lines."

"But why do we have to straighten out our lines?" Hodges asked, mystified by Monty's order.

"Because you can't win a big victory without a tidy show."

Hodges stared at Monty as if Monty had just stepped off a spaceship from Mars. "But sir, those positions might be useful when it comes time to launch our counterattack."

"I don't think so," Monty replied. "That salient is messy and dangerous. First we must sort out the battlefield and tidy up our lines, and then we'll counterattack. Do you have anything else to report?"

"No, sir—I don't think so."

"Very well, then. Good day."

Monty turned around and marched out of the office, followed by his aides. Supremely confident, his shoulders thrown back, he made his way out of the building to his command car, got in, and was driven away. GIs on the street recognized his famous face and red beret and waved. "Hiya Monty!" they shouted.

"Hello boys!" he replied, giving them thumbs up.

Mahoney had spent the night on the barricades, freezing his ass. In the morning, the paratrooper unit he had fought with was relieved, and he thought he'd better get some sleep someplace because he'd been on the go for three days in a row.

He had no idea of where to sack out because he'd never been assigned to a permanent unit. He decided that his best bet would be to return to General McAuliffe's headquarters and find a cozy little nook there because the chances were that they'd have a fire going and it would be warm.

He dragged himself through the streets of Bastogne, his head aching from lack of sleep, and the city looked even worse than it had the day before. More buildings had been blown up, and more streets were impassable. Mahoney knew they couldn't hold out much longer. If help didn't come from someplace, they'd be slaughtered.

He was so sleepy that he walked into a broken telephone pole and knocked himself senseless. When he opened his eyes, he was on his knees with his shoulder lodged against the telephone pole. I can't go on like this, he thought. I've got to lie down someplace.

Looking around, he saw a partially destroyed building. A little tin chimney had been rigged through one of the walls, and smoke wafted out of it. Mahoney staggered into the building and descended into the cellar, where a group of civilians were huddled around a small potbellied stove. They made room for Mahoney at the stove, but he found a vacant corner, collapsed into it, and closed his eyes. In seconds, he was snoring loudly.

The Hammerhead Division continued its drive to the north through little towns and vast expanses of farm country. The men of Charlie Company rode on the lead tanks, and shortly after twelve noon another village was spotted in the distance. The tank column slowed down and came to a stop.

The commander of the tank which Cranepool and his squad were riding on peered at the town through his binoculars.

"What are we stopping for?" Cranepool asked.

"There's supposed to be krauts in that town."

The tanks stayed in place while word was passed back to General Hughes that the lead tank column was approaching a town held by the Germans. The commander of the tank units requested instructions on how to take the town.

General Hughes was riding in a jeep about midpoint in the column when the message came through on the radio. He didn't have to think about it much because he'd been with Patton long enough to know that speed and surprise were the most important elements of success.

"We're not going to waste any time in that town," he told the tank commander. "Just go right through it with guns blazing, and don't stop for anything."

"What about the infantry on my tanks, sir?"

"You just leave them right where they are. Infantry soldiers would rather ride than walk no matter what the circumstances are."

General Hughes's orders were passed back and forth along the armored column, and finally they arrived in the tank on which Cranepool was riding.

"Well," said the tank commander, a lieutenant named Pellegrini, "you guys had better hang on tight because our orders are to roll through the town as quickly as we can with all guns blazing."

Cranepool tipped his helmet back and tried to figure out the implications of the order. He realized that he and his men would be sitting ducks atop the tank, and they wouldn't be able to fight back because they'd be too busy trying to hang on.

"All right you guys!" he shouted, as the tank revved up its engine. "I want all of you to take off your belts and tie yourselves to this tank, so you can use your weapons when we get into that town."

The tank column moved forward. Cranepool's men worked feverishly to yank off their belts and strap themselves to the various fittings on the tank. Cranepool fastened his left thigh to the turret and positioned himself on one knee. The tank bounced up and down as it gathered speed over the icy road, and Cranepool wrapped his carbine sling around his left arm so he wouldn't drop it by mistake.

The tank column with the Hammerheads aboard roared down the incline toward the town. The Germans saw them coming and got set behind their main defensive line, but there weren't too many Germans because Hitler had deployed the weight of his Ardennes offensive to the center and north, while his southern flank consisted almost entirely of infantry, and they were spread out all over Belgium.

The tank column approached the barricade at the edge of town, and Cranepool felt the cold wind bite into his face and whistle through his epaulettes. The lead tanks raked the barricades with machine gun fire and shot their cannons at it. The Germans hadn't been in the town very long and hadn't time to build substantial fortifications, so after several volleys, a path was blasted through the barricade.

The air filled with bullets flying in all directions. Cranepool kneeled on the rocking tank and fired his carbine on automatic at the barricade that was coming closer every moment. The lead tanks broke through and kept going at top speed. Cranepool and his men were on the fifth tank, and as it approached the barricade, Cranepool took out a hand grenade, pulled the pin, waited until he was abreast of the barricade, and hurled it at the Germans.

The grenade sailed through the air, and Cranepool lost his balance, falling to his side on the hard cold metal, but the belt on his leg kept him from rolling down the side of the tank. The grenade exploded, killing three Germans. Cranepool righted himself again, looked up, and saw German helmets in the windows of the one and two story buildings that lined the street. He and his men fired at the Germans as the tanks sped through the town, roaring around corners and accelerating down the straightaways. Germans toppled off the roofs and out of the windows of buildings as the tankers fired their machine guns and the infantry soldiers shot them with rifles. The Hammerheads threw hand grenades through windows, and some of them even managed to fire bazookas from atop moving tanks.

The Germans fired their anti-tank guns at the column of tanks, knocking several out of action. The soldiers atop them were killed instantly by the explosions, but the column continued to roll through the town.

Then, the tank in front of Cranepool's took a direct hit, and flying shrapnel killed Private Sequira instantly. Lieutenant Pellegrini kept going, crashed into the destroyed tank, and pushed it out of the way. A German behind some bushes aimed his *panzerfaust* (an anti-tank weapon) at the tank and fired it, but the shell fell short, exploding and splattering Cranepool and his men with stones and dust. Private Richardson was hit in the forehead with one of the stones, and its force cracked open his skull. He collapsed onto the tank but didn't fall off it because he'd tied himself to its ammunition rack. His blood trickled onto the o.d. green paint and dripped into the moving treads as the tank accelerated forward.

Cranepool held his carbine tight to his waist and sprayed buildings with automatic fire as the tank sped through the village. The tank turned a corner, and he glanced ahead to see the open road again. He fired a last burst of bullets at two Germans on a rooftop, and then his carbine went empty. He ejected the empty clip, slapped in a new one, and when he looked up again, his tank had cleared the village and was rolling through the countryside again.

On the lee side of a white Tiger King tank, General Fritz Bayerlein studied the map of Bastogne and tried to figure out tactics for taking the stubborn city. The cold wind whistled around him, carrying flakes of snow. Sergeant Kriesler mumbled into the field telephone, then turned to Bayerlein.

"It's Field Marshal Model, sir."

Bayerlein took the telephone, groaning softly because he knew he was going to be chewed out. "Bayerlein here," he said.

"Bayerlein," said Model, "the Fuehrer is furious over your inability to take Bastogne. It is inconceivable to him, and I must confess even to me, that you have not taken it yet, in view of your superiority in terms of numbers of tanks and men."

"Sir," Bayerlein replied, "the enemy has had time to build a strong defensive position in Bastogne, and they're fighting like wild animals. Whenever we attack, we're met with a wall of tanks."

"Where are you attacking from?"

"The east, sir."

"That's what I thought. Why don't you sideslip around the city and attack from the south? You might be able to surprise them that way, and I suggest you send infantry in first to clear a way for the tanks, since you're not having much luck the other way around. Do you think that might work?"

"It's worth a try, sir. They must be running low on food and ammunition. They'll have to crack sooner or later."

"I hope it's sooner, for your sake, Bayerlein. That is all."

Bayerlein handed the phone back to Sergeant Kriesler and looked at the map again as he planned his new attack from the south.

Colonel James O'Neill, the chaplain of the Third Army, knocked on the door of Patton's office.

"Come in!" said the voice inside.

Chaplain O'Neill entered the office, approched General

Patton at his desk, and saluted awkwardly. "You wanted to see me, sir?"

"Yes, I did," said Patton. "Have a seat."

"Yes, sir."

O'Neill sat on one of the chairs in front of Patton's desk. He was a white haired man with fine, sensitive features, and he wondered what Patton wanted from him this time.

"Chaplain O'Neill," said Patton, "I have a very important mission for you, but I have complete confidence that you'll carry it out to the best of your ability. As you know, we're attacking the Germans to the north of us, but we're not moving as fast as I'd like because we don't have air support, and we don't have air support because the weather's been atrocious. Therefore, when you leave this office, I want you to go to some quiet secluded spot and pray for good flying weather."

Chaplain O'Neill didn't know whether Patton was joking with him or not. "Sir," he said, "it's going to take an awfully thick rug for that kind of praying."

"I don't care if it takes a flying carpet," Patton replied. "I want the praying done."

"But sir, it isn't customary for men of my profession to pray for clear weather so that people can kill each other more effectively."

Patton pointed his finger at Chaplain O'Neill. "Are you here to teach me theology, or are you the chaplain of the Third Army?"

"I'm chaplain of the Third Army, sir."

"Then get out of here, and start praying!"

"Yes, sir."

Chaplain O'Neill stood, saluted, and marched out of Patton's office. He made his way to his little chapel, knelt before the cross, and prayed for clear weather just as Patton had ordered him to do. Chaplain O'Neill couldn't help feeling ridiculous, but orders were orders, and he obeyed like a good soldier.

FIFTEEN

Mahoney was awakened by the sound of a ferocious explosion. He opened his eyes and looked around as bits of the ceiling fell down and the people in the cellar screamed in panic. Mahoney grabbed his rifle and stood, squinting and trying to see the doorway through the clouds of dust. He held one hand in front of him and made his way to the door, passing through the outside corridor and climbing the stairs.

He heard a great number of artillery shells falling in his vicinity and knew the Germans must be attacking again. Leaving the building, he saw that it was dawn and the street in front of him was filled with paratroopers running toward the center of the city. Looking to his left, he saw a horde of German soldiers coming round the bend.

He realized in an instant that the Germans had broken through someplace. An empty American armored personnel carrier fleeing down the middle of the street was hit by a German anti-tank shell, and its rear end was blown to shreds. Its driver jumped out of the cab and ran away.

Mahoney charged into the street, "Hold on!" he shouted to the fleeing paratroopers. "Stand your ground!"

But the paratroopers kept running. Their defensive lines had been breached, and they were falling back to new positions, although they couldn't afford to give up much ground in a small, surrounded city like Bastogne.

Bullets ricocheted off the street and whizzed through the air as Mahoney tried to think of what to do. His eyes fell on the .50 caliber machine gun on top of the destroyed armored personnel carrier. It might be working, and if it was, it could stop the Germans long enough for the paratroopers to regroup and counterattack.

Mahoney ran into the street, pushing paratroopers out of

his way. He leapt onto the back of the vehicle, climbed over the wreckage, and made his way to the .50 caliber machine gun on the roof of the cab. He looked it over, and it appeared undamaged. Leaning his rifle against the wall of the tiny enclosed spot where the machine gun had been mounted, he saw that the machine gun was loaded and that there were three crates of bullets on the floor.

Mahoney swung the machine gun around and looked down the sights at German soldiers swarming down the street toward him. He prayed the machine gun would work and pressed the thumb triggers. It fired thunderously, and the big bullets blasted out of the barrel. The bullets were almost twice the size of ordinary rifle or machine gun bullets and were designed to shoot down planes and pierce light armor. Each fifth bullet was a tracer so the gunner could see where he was firing.

Mahoney held the triggers down and swung the machine gun from side to side on its transverse mechanism. A hail of bullets illuminated by tracers flew down the street and ripped into the Germans, who were jammed together between the buildings that lined the street. The bullets were so powerful they could go through three or four Germans before they ran out of steam, and the front wall of attacking Germans collapsed before the hot lead, blood spurting out of their bodies.

Mahoney kept firing, the big machine gun shaking his entire body, and he shot down the second wave of Germans. But the rest of them kept coming. They were enthusiastic and felt heroic because they'd managed to storm the city's outer defenses, but Mahoney's bullets tore them apart and soon heaps of dead Germans lay in the street. The attack faltered.

Mahoney stopped a moment to give the machine gun a rest. "COME ON YOU COCKSUCKERS!" he screamed. "IF YOU WANT A FIGHT—HERE I AM!"

A German hiding behind a telephone pole fired a *panzerfaust* at the armored vehicle, and it hit low in back, blowing apart the metal armor and rear axle and jolting Mahoney so badly he was thrown against the wall of his little machine gun nest. His head would have been bashed in if he hadn't been wearing a helmet, but he pulled himself together quickly and got behind the machine gun again.

Pressing the thumb triggers, the machine gun kicked and trembled on its stalk. In the corner of his eye, he saw some Germans trying to set up an anti-tank gun, so he swung the machine gun in that direction and poured lead into them until they all were lying on the ground with enormous holes in their bodies.

The German with the *panzerfaust* fired again, but this time his aim was wide, and his shell flew past the left side of Mahoney. However, Mahoney had seen him fire the weapon. Mahoney aimed his machine gun at the hapless German and directed a deadly stream of bullets at him. The German tried to hide himself behind the telephone pole, but the big bullets ripped the wood apart, and one bullet finally slammed into the German's chest, knocking him off his feet. The rest of the bullets cut the telephone pole in half, causing the top half to fall on the dead German and break his bones.

The retreating American paratroopers saw what Mahoney was doing, and realized they had a chance against the Germans after all. They stopped running, took cover, and fired back at the Germans. Their sergeants and officers reestablished order and moved the men forward, utilizing the principles of fire and maneuver. Machine guns and bazookas were put into position.

Atop the ruined personnel carrier, Mahoney fired the machine gun until he came to the end of the belt, and it flew off into the air. Bending down, he opened the second crate of ammunition and fed the fresh belt into the chamber. As he was standing, a German anti-tank shell hit the personnel carrier, and once again he was thrown to the side by the explosion.

He regained consciousness with a terrible headache and blood oozing out of a cut on his forehead. Staggering to his feet, he heard tank engines, and turned to see one of General McAuliffe's roving tank units tearing down the street. The American paratroopers made way, and the tanks passed Mahoney, charging toward the German soldiers, who scattered in all directions and ran to safety. The tanks fired their cannons and machine guns at the Germans, and when they caught up with them, they knocked them to the ground and rolled over them.

The American paratroopers shouted and bellowed as they brandished their rifles and ran to mop up what remained of the Germans. Mahoney slung his rifle over his shoulder and climbed down from the ruined personnel carrier. Standing beside it, he lit a cigarette and wondered where to go for breakfast. Then he remembered Madeleine at the hospital. He looked at his watch. It was eight o'clock in the morning. Maybe she was on duty now!

Mahoney oriented himself and set off in the direction of the hospital, thinking of Madeleine and her frail beauty. He yearned to gather her into his arms and kiss her curvaceous lips, but after that, he couldn't imagine what he'd do. He thought that to screw such a creature would be like a violation of the pure food act. There was something pristine and wonderful about her despite her profession. She only did that to stay alive, but he knew she was no whore at heart. He believed that despite all the soldiers she'd been to bed with, the essential part of her remained pure and always would be pure. He saw her face before him and began to run. Paratroopers moving about on the streets saw him and figured he was carrying a message of the utmost importance.

Finally, he came to the civilian hospital, which had been hit by several more shells since he had seen it last. He went inside, and it was more crowded than before, with wounded people stacked like sardines in the reception room and corridors. Mahoney stepped over their bodies as he made his way to the children's ward.

It too had become more crowded, and the chubby woman with big boobs was on duty. Some of the children noticed Mahoney, and their big eyes widened.

"Hey GI," one of them said. "You got candy for me?"

Mahoney felt embarrassed because he knew he should have brought something for the children, but he'd been thinking only of Madeleine.

"Sorry kiddo," Mahoney said cheerily. "Next time I come, I'll have some candy for everybody."

As the words left his mouth, he wondered where he was going to get candy for all these kids. The chubby woman saw him and walked toward him in the narrow space between the beds.

"Hello," she said with a smile. "You've come to see Madeleine?"

"Yes, is she around?"

"She's in the pharmacy. I'll go get her for you."

The woman walked away. Mahoney took off his helmet and tried to think of something clever to say to Madeleine when she showed up. He racked his brain for a suitable line, but nothing came to him. I guess I'll just say hello, he thought. I'll ask her how she's been doing.

He began to worry that she wouldn't remember him. Maybe she hadn't even liked him and had been friendly because that was her job. She might not even be in this hospital. It might be another Madeleine, and his Madeleine might have left Bastogne before it was surrounded.

He heard footsteps behind him and turned around. His heart sank as he saw a brunette around Madeleine's height, but it wasn't Madeleine. Oh shit, he thought, I knew it all was too good to be true. This is a different Madeleine.

The woman wore a wrinkled dress and looked exhausted, but she tried to smile. "May I help you?" she asked.

"No, that's all right," Mahoney replied, shuffling toward the door.

"Are you sure?"

"Yes ma'am. Thanks anyway."

Mahoney turned to walk away, feeling sick and demoralized.

"Hey GI!" yelled one of the kids. "Don't forget the candy next time!"

"I won't!" Mahoney replied.

Mahoney shuffled sadly through the hospital, thinking that Madeleine had slipped through his fingers, and he'd never see her again. But at least he could get some candy for the kids. I think she would have wanted me to do that, he thought.

The hospital's pharmacy was located in its basement, and the chubby woman, whose name was Jeanette, found the Madeleine that Mahoney had been looking for in the long line.

"Madeleine!" said Jeanette. "That big soldier I told you about is up in the ward looking for you!"

Madeleine's eyes lit with joy. "Right now?"

"Yes! I'll take your place in line! Go up, and see him!"

Smiling happily, Madeleine ran from the pharmacy and

headed for the stairs. When she'd learned that Mahoney had come looking for her yesterday, she'd thought it marvelous because he'd been on her mind ever since that night in the café in Clervaux. She'd thought him extraordinarily handsome, resembling the American actor John Garfield somewhat, and he'd been so sweet and charming, not vulgar like most of the other GIs. He'd fought for her honor, on top of everything else. No man ever had done that for her before. She couldn't wait to see him again.

She flew up the staircase, wondering what to say to him. At first she thought of saying, "Hiya—I see you've come back for your five dollars' worth," or something else clever like that, but no, that would be a whore's remark, and she didn't want to be a whore anymore. She'd felt useful since she'd been working in the hospital and intended to continue there as long as they'd let her.

She reached the main floor of the hospital and raced toward the children's ward. I'll just be honest with him, she thought. I'll say, "Hello—I'm glad to see you again." That ought to do it. He's a man and he'll be able to take it from there.

As she neared the children's ward, her heart beat like a drum. She felt a mad tickle in her stomach, and her mouth was dry with anxiety. She charged into the children's ward, looked around, and saw only Annette with the children.

"Where is he?" Madeleine asked Annette.

Annette was washing the face of a little girl. "Where's who?"

Madeleine's brown eyes darted all over the ward. "The American soldier who was just here!"

"Oh him? He left."

"He left!" screamed Madeleine.

Annette looked at Madeleine. "Yes, he left. What's wrong?"

"Where did he go?"

"How should I know?"

"Didn't he say anything?"

"I asked if I could help him, and he said he was sorry, and walked away."

"What!"

Annette narrowed her eyes at Madeleine. "What's wrong with you, dear?"

Madeleine sighed, closed her eyes, and pressed the palm of

her hand against her forehead, wondering why Mahoney had walked away and whether or not he'd ever return.

Mahoney was melancholy and had lost his appetite. Wearily he climbed the steps to General McAuliffe's headquarters and entered the building. He made his way through the corridors and finally arrived at the conference room.

General McAuliffe stood around the table with his top commanders and aides. Mahoney joined them silently and soon learned that the situation had become perilous in Bastogne. The 101st Airborne was low on artillery ammunition, and some cannons only had one or two shells left to fire. There was also a shortage of regular ammunition, and not much food was left.

"Sir," said an officer at the table, "we simply can't hold out much longer."

"Baloney!" said General McAuliffe. "We'll hold out even if we have to throw snowballs at the bastards."

"If only the weather would clear," somebody said. "Then we could be resupplied by air."

"Well," replied McAuliffe, "I wouldn't count on that if I were you. This weather we're having looks like it's going to continue for quite some time."

"Sir," said a major, "maybe a few men in trucks could break out of here at night, get some supplies, and come back."

McAuliffe shook his head. "Too risky."

"We wouldn't be risking much, sir, and if we succeeded, our situation here would be considerably improved. I could ask for volunteers."

"Well," said McAuliffe, "I want you to make it clear to the volunteers that the mission is a real longshot."

"I'll do that sir, and I'll lead it myself."

McAuliffe looked at the map. "Let's see what the best direction would be for you to go."

All the officers looked down at the map and pondered the matter.

"I'd say," said McAuliffe, "that your best chance would be on a road heading south."

Mahoney cleared his throat. "I was on that road yesterday, sir, and there were Germans all over it."

"Can we go north?" asked McAuliffe.

"Too many Germans to the north, sir," said a colonel. "That's where the bulk of their forces are."

"How about to the east?"

"That's no good either," said a captain. "Eighth Corps reports that there's a wall of Germans between them and us."

"Hmmm," said the major, looking at the map. "You said you were on that southern road yesterday, Sergeant?"

"Yes, sir. In the morning."

The major looked at General McAuliffe. "The picture on that road might have changed drastically since yesterday morning, sir. Patton is attacking from the south, and it's highly possible that troops have been pulled off that road and moved farther south to fight him."

"You might be right, Johnny," McAuliffe said. "If you want to try it, you have my permission, but don't take more than three trucks and six men."

"Thank you sir," the major said, and then turned to Mahoney. "Since you were on that road yesterday, you must know it pretty well. Care to come along and help us out?"

Fucked again, Mahoney thought, but he smiled and said, "Yes, sir."

SIXTEEN

It was one o'clock in the morning, and three deuce and a half trucks rolled through Bastogne. In the lead truck was Mahoney, with Pfc Steven Ball of Casper, Wyoming, behind the wheel. The paratrooper major, whose name was Strickland, rode in the second truck.

The three trucks headed toward the south of town. The plan

was to leave not by the road but over the frozen fields to the woods and then through the woods for a few miles until they thought they'd passed the main German lines. Then they'd head for the road and try to break through to the south.

Each of them was armed with a Thompson submachine gun, and each had been issued a map of the area and a compass in case there was trouble and they had to split up.

They reached the edge of the town, and all was silent except for an occasional artillery shell or machine gun burst. The night was pitch black, but if they headed due south, they'd hit the woods before long. They drove off the road and onto the frozen crust of the field, moving along slowly in low gear so they wouldn't make too much noise.

The trucks rolled across the field, and Mahoney hoped they wouldn't hit a weak spot in the snow and fall through. But the temperature was twenty-five degrees, and the snow held. Mahoney and the paratroopers looked around for signs of Germans and expected to draw German fire at any moment, but suddenly trees loomed up in front of them, and they knew they'd made it to the woods.

Mahoney got out of the lead truck and walked in front of it to guide the trucks through the trees, which were tall and spaced far apart. Major Strickland replaced Mahoney in the front seat of the lead truck, and Mahoney moved through the forest, holding his submachine gun ready and walking slowly enough so that Pfc Ball could see him.

The forest was dark and eerie. Mahoney's sharp eyes picked out the black forms of trees against the gray snow and he threaded his way among them, listening for odd sounds and straining to see the shape of a German helmet or the gleam of a German button.

A bird leapt into the air a few yards away from Mahoney, and Mahoney almost fired a burst at it but realized in time that it was only a partridge or quail flapping its wings and trying to escape from the weird caravan. Adrenaline pumped through Mahoney's arteries, and his mouth was dry even though the bird could be heard no more. He stooped down, picked up a chunk of snow from a bush, and put it into his mouth.

Fifteen minutes passed, and Mahoney gradually became

more confident. He thought it might actually be possible for them to get around the main body of Germans and then roll onto the road when suddenly he heard a *crack* to his front, the sound a foot makes when it comes down on a branch and breaks it.

Mahoney held up his hand, and the trucks stopped. He moved his hand to the side in a cutting motion, and the drivers turned off their engines. Straining his ears, he listened for sounds and wondered if the wood had snapped because of the intense cold or whether someone was out there.

He heard footsteps on the snow somewhere to his front, and his blood turned to ice. Then he heard something moving past a bush. He held out his arms like Christ on the cross, and the paratroopers silently climbed down from the trucks.

Major Strickland eased toward Mahoney. "What's up?" he whispered.

"Somebody's out there," Mahoney whispered back.

"Are you sure?"

A machine gun opened fire in front of them, and Major Strickland's question was answered. Bullets zipped through the air, clanging against the trucks, and everybody dropped to the ground. One of the paratroopers was hit in the neck, and the impact of the bullet nearly tore his head off before he landed.

Mahoney raised his submachine gun to his shoulder and prepared to fire back, but Major Strickland slapped down the barrel of the gun.

"Don't fire!" Strickland said. "You'll give away our position!"

"You think they don't know our position?"

"They'll know it a damn sight better if you give them a muzzle blast to zero in on."

Another German machine gun opened fire, and then numerous rifles joined in. The air above Mahoney's head became thick with bullets, and he knew that the mission had failed already, that it had been a harebrained idea to begin with and now they had to get out of there.

The other paratroopers crawled toward Mahoney and Strickland. Mahoney peered ahead at the muzzle blasts of the German weapons and thought a few bursts of submachine gun fire might quiet them down for awhile.

"Sir," said Mahoney, "they're going to rush us before long. I think we'd better get out of here."

"I'm trying to figure out whether we should split up or try to go back together."

"I think we should split up, sir. We'll make too much noise together."

Machine gun bullets kicked up snow in front of Mahoney and the paratroopers.

"Let's go, sir!" Mahoney said with urgency. "Make up your mind!"

"All right men!" Strickland replied. "We're going back in two groups." He explained that Mahoney would leave with Pfc Ball, and he'd go with the other two paratroopers. "We'll throw some hand grenades to cover our movements. All right now—get ready."

They took out hand grenades and pulled the pins, looking at Strickland for the command to throw them.

"NOW!" he yelled.

They all hurled their hand grenades toward the muzzle blasts of the German guns, and seconds later the night was torn apart by fiery orange explosions. Trees crashed to the ground, Germans screamed, and Major Strickland yelled, "MOVE OUT!"

Mahoney and the paratroopers jumped up and ran toward Bastogne. The Germans recovered from the grenade attack and sprayed the woods with machine gun bullets. Mahoney ran beside Pfc Ball and suddenly Ball screamed and tumbled to the ground. Mahoney dived head first into some bushes, but there was a tree behind them, and he crashed into it head first. If he hadn't had his helmet on, he would have split his head open, but instead he only knocked himself out for a few seconds.

He opened his eyes and realized he was lying on the snow. Pfc Ball lay moaning and bleeding only a few feet away. German bullets whistled through the woods, and Mahoney crawled to Ball, who lay on his stomach, his back a mass of blood. Ball's eyes were closed, and he was unconscious but moaning softly anyway.

Mahoney realized he couldn't do anything for Ball but maybe he could save his own ass. He slithered away as quickly as he could, hearing the German bullets crackle over his head and wham into trees nearby. He continued crawling, came to a little gully, and dropped into it.

The Germans stopped firing suddenly, and he heard a German order that his men advance cautiously. Seconds later Mahoney heard footsteps and the rustling of bushes, which he thought might cover his own escape. Crouching low, he held his submachine gun tightly and moved north, bringing his feet down silently, and being careful not to brush against any branches. He heard the Germans talking and learned that they'd found some bodies. Mahoney wondered if Major Strickland had gotten away.

Mahoney continued walking cautiously through the woods. Every ten steps, he'd stop and listen for several seconds and then move out again. The German voices behind him sounded farther away, and after a while, he could barely hear them.

He congratulated himself for having escaped. Now all he had to do was make it back to Bastogne in one piece. He craved a cigarette but didn't dare smoke. Thinking about what had happened, he concluded that the Germans must have had some patrols in the woods, and one of them had heard the convoy. That meant he'd have to be extra careful so that he didn't bump into any more Germans.

Slowly, he made his way through the woods. He estimated that he should be back in Bastogne in two or three hours if no problems developed.

Mahoney couldn't see well in the darkness, and he tripped over a branch, tumbling head over heels into a ditch.

"Is that you, Hans?" asked a voice in German.

Mahoney looked up and saw a big hulk of a man a few feet away in the ditch. He didn't dare shoot the German soldier because it would attract too much attention, so he reached for the bayonet on his belt.

"Hans?" asked the German soldier.

Mahoney pulled out his bayonet and leapt toward the German soldier. He covered the German's mouth with his big hand and pushed the bayonet with all his might into the German's belly. The German twisted his face away from Mahoney's hand and howled in pain. Mahoney slashed his throat, and the howling stopped.

"What's going on over there!" asked another German voice.

Mahoney picked up his submachine gun and jumped out of the ditch. He ran into the woods in a crouch and heard Germans shouting behind him. They fired a few shots, but the bullets came nowhere near Mahoney.

He ran for several minutes, dodging around trees and jumping over bushes. Then he stopped to catch his breath and listen for sound of pursuit. All he heard was a commotion in the distance behind him. He grinned when he realized that the Germans probably thought they'd been infiltrated by an American patrol and were shooting at shadows.

He continued moving again and happened to look up at the sky. Something twinkled up there, and he blinked to make sure he wasn't imagining things. It still twinkled and Mahoney realized it was a star!

That meant the weather was clearing, and he wanted to jump for joy, but instead he kept himself under control and stepped over the snow, still heading for Bastogne.

SEVENTEEN

Chaplain O'Neill awoke to the sound of a tremendous roar over his head. He opened his eyes and saw sunlight streaming through the flaps of his tent. Rolling out of bed, he stuck his feet into his boots, put on his field jacket and helmet, and went outside.

He looked up and saw the sky blanketed with American airplanes. The weather had cleared, and for the first time, the American Air Force was going after the Germans in the bulge. He recalled his prayer yesterday, and being a religious soul, was thunderstruck by the thought that his prayer had brought this about. The Lord had heard him and delivered good weather. He was about to fall down and offer thanks, when he realized the theological implications: there would be widespread death and destruction today because of him.

As he was pondering this, he saw General Patton walking toward him across the tent encampment. Patton was resplendent in polished boots, a neatly pressed uniform, and his pearl-handled revolver at his hip.

"Good morning, Chaplain O'Neill," Patton said, holding out his hand and smiling broadly. "I just wanted to shake your hand and thank you for making the sun come out. I have always believed in the power of prayer, and now I believe more than ever. You sure must stand in good with the Lord."

Patton shook Chaplain O'Neill's hand, and the chaplain tried to smile.

As Mahoney approached Bastogne, he saw cargo planes dropping huge bundles of supplies. The ground shook beneath his feet from the tons of bombs falling on Germans in the vicinity, and vast clouds of smoke darkened the day.

He thought the supplies ought to contain some candy and realized that it was the day before Christmas. Somehow he'd have to get some of that candy and give it to the kids in the hospital. He remembered their big eyes and sad faces and quickened his step.

He entered the city of Bastogne, and there was jubilation everywhere as paratroopers hauled the newly arrived supplies to the places where they were needed. The situation had seemed bleak only a few hours ago, but now, everything had changed.

Mahoney made his way to the headquarters of the 101st Airborne, checked the conference room, and found it empty.

"Where's General McAuliffe?" he asked a private in the hall.

"In his office, I think."

Mahoney proceeded to General McAuliffe's office, stated his name to the general's clerk, and was told to go right in.

General McAuliffe sat behind his desk, looking over reports from his various front-line positions. "Mahoney!" he said. "You're back already? What happened?"

Mahoney sat in a chair. "We ran smack into some Germans, and as far as I know, I'm the only survivor."

McAuliffe frowned. "Damn," he said. He closed his eyes and shook his head. "Damn."

"Well, at least we got resupplied by air today."

McAuliffe opened his eyes. "Yes. And just in time, too. I don't think we could have made it through the day otherwise. Well, I've got to get back to work, Mahoney. Why don't you get something to eat and sack out for awhile."

"Sir, I'd like to ask you a favor if I may."

"Shoot," said McAuliffe.

"Well, sir," Mahoney began, "I happened to be in the civilian hospital here a few days ago, and they've got a ward full of the most pathetic bunch of kids you've ever seen in your life. I thought that since it was Christmas tomorrow, you might let me get some candy from your G-4 officer so's I can bring it to the kids."

McAuliffe smiled, and Mahoney realized it was the first time he'd ever seen him do that. "That sounds like a nice idea," McAuliffe said. "Go ahead and do it, and if anybody gives you any trouble, just refer them to me."

It was noon at SHAEF Headquarters in Versailles, and the morning conference had just finished. Ike stood alone in front of the map table, and for the first time since the German offensive had begun, he felt no anxiety.

Reports indicated that the American Air Force was pulverizing the Germans from the air while increasing numbers of American units were being brought to bear against the Germans on the ground. It was believed that the German offensive was coming to a standstill. Patton's Third Army was hitting the Germans hard in the south while Monty's forces were holding fast in the north and were on the verge of launching a huge counteroffensive. Germans were abandoning their tanks because they had run out of fuel. One battalion strength German panzer unit had nearly reached the Meuse River, but the American Second Armored Division was on the way to head it off.

Ike looked down at the city of Bastogne. That was the only serious problem left. The garrison was still surrounded and could conceivably be wiped out. The Third Army was driving toward Bastogne from the south, and Ike hoped it would arrive on time.

He decided to put an immediate call through to Patton and tell him to make Bastogne his number one priority.

EIGHTEEN

It was Christmas Eve in Bastogne and the fighting had diminished to an occasional shot from a rifle or a burst of machine gun fire. American soldiers sang Christmas carols in their trenches and bunkers while in the distance they heard German soldiers singing along in their own language. Stars blazed across the sky, and religious services were held on both sides of no-man's-land.

Mahoney and a group of paratroopers moved through the streets of the city, carrying bags of food and candy, and one of them lugged an eight foot pine tree that he'd cut down in the woods.

Mahoney puffed a cigarette and hummed "Jingle Bells" as he recalled the Christmases of his youth, waking up early in the morning and rushing to the Christmas tree to get his presents. Never had he anticipated anything as much as Christmas even though, year after year, he received cheap things like coloring books and cookies or maybe some clothes that he needed because his family was poor.

He and his parents, and his younger brother and sister, never missed Mass on Christmas day, and the priest always said they shouldn't forget that Christmas was not just for giving and receiving presents, but was the birthday of Jesus Christ, the Prince of Peace.

Mahoney snorted sardonically when he remembered that, because he'd had no peace for almost three years and had seen incredible bloodshed and brutality during that time. Yet, although Americans and Germans were only a few hundred yards apart in Bastogne and had been fighting each other viciously for the past several days, there was peace in Bastogne tonight. Soldiers, who on other evenings would be trying to kill each other, were singing about the little town in Bethlehem, remembering Christmases of years past, and praying that they'd be alive on Christmases to come.

If we all could be good Christians, Mahoney thought, there would be no more wars, but it's too hard to be a good Christian and be loving toward people you can't stand and turn the other cheek when people like the Nazis start pushing you around and throwing people into concentration camps. The Bible says there is a time for war and a time for peace, and it looks like this is the time for war.

They reached the hospital, and Mahoney led the paratroopers inside. Priests walked among the sick, blessing them and saying prayers. Candles flickered in the gloom, and somewhere in the hospital, a group of people was singing "O Come All Ye Faithful."

Mahoney stopped the paratroopers outside the children's ward, and they set down their bundles, taking out false white beards they'd made from bed sheets torn into strips and held together by safety pins. They tied the beards on and looked at each other, realizing they appeared ridiculous, but it was Christmas Eve and so what?

They gathered together and picked up their bundles. Mahoney slung his over his shoulder and strolled into the ward. "Merry Christmas kids!" he said in a deep booming voice. "Ho ho ho!"

The kids turned around and stared at him, then burst into smiles. They knew exactly who he was and held out their hands.

"Gimme some candy, GI!" they said. "Hey—over here, GI!"

"GI?" Mahoney replied. "I'm not a GI! I'm Santa Claus, and these are my helpers!"

"Then how come you're wearing an Army uniform?" one of them asked.

"Because my regular clothes are in the laundry."

Annette was working in the ward, and she recognized Mahoney in an instant. She walked toward him, a big smile on her face. "Merry Christmas!" she said.

"Ho ho ho," Mahoney replied. "Merry Christmas to you

too! Do you mind if me and my helpers give some stuff to the kids?"

"Go right ahead," she said. "But please don't let any of them eat too much and get sick."

"Oh no, we wouldn't do that! Ho ho ho!"

Mahoney and the paratroopers passed out candy and peanut butter sandwiches, and the eyes of the children sparkled with happiness. Their tiny hands flailed the air as they tried to attract the attention of the soldiers, and they squealed with delight. The paratroopers made funny faces and acted silly although they'd been an elite bunch of killers only a few hours ago.

"Ho ho ho!" said Mahoney, pressing a chocolate bar into the hand of a little girl. "God bless us every one!"

Annette ran to the canteen in the basement, and saw Madeleine drinking coffee with some other aides. "Madeleine," Annette said excitedly, "he's back!"

Madeleine knew instantly who she was talking about. "He's in the ward?"

"Yes! Hurry!"

Madeleine wanted to run as fast as she could, but she didn't want to appear ludicrous to her co-workers, so she walked swiftly out of the canteen and climbed the flight of stairs to the main floor of the hospital. Something had told her that he'd return sooner or later, and now he had.

She came to the ward and saw chaos. The children who were ambulatory had gotten out of bed and were climbing all over the soldiers, who looked absurd with strips of white cloth hanging from their faces. One soldier was hammering nails into a stand which would hold a pine tree, whose fragrance could be smelled through the odor of medicine and disinfectant. Then her eyes fell on him, his beard crooked on his face because a child was pulling it as he bent over the child's bed, a chocolate bar in his hand.

She clasped her hands behind her back and walked toward him. He caught her movement in the corner of his eye and turned around. His heart beat like a big gong as he recognized her, and his jaw dropped open. The child snatched the chocolate bar out of his hand, and then pulled away his beard.

She smiled and stopped in front of him. "Hello," she said. "I heard you came by a few days ago to see me."

Mahoney told himself to snap out of it as he gazed at her features, especially the alluring shape of her lips. "Yes, but I thought you weren't here."

"Well, I'm here."

They looked at each other, and there was nothing more to say. She fell into his arms, and he held her tight, kissing her forehead. He wanted to tell her that he was overjoyed to see her, and she wanted to say she would have died if he hadn't returned, but then their lips met, and they said it all silently.

South of Bastogne, the Hammerhead Division had stopped for the night, and the men sat on the snow near tanks and ate C rations while thinking of their families and friends back in the States celebrating Christmas Eve without them.

In Charlie Company, Captain Anderson threw his poncho over his head and shined his flashlight on the map spread out on his knees, trying to study in advance the terrain over which they'd fight tomorrow. He tried not to think about home because it was too painful for him. He was only twenty-two years old, and he missed his parents and his girlfriend, whom he was engaged to marry. Every time there was a mail call, he expected her to return his ring along with a Dear John letter, but she hadn't done it yet, thank goodness. He didn't know if he could handle it if she did.

So he tried to bury himself in the terrain shown on the map. He measured the distance to Bastogne and thought they might get there in another two or three days if the Germans didn't put up too much resistance. Today's advance had been much easier, thanks to the air support. Trucks had been brought up from the rear because too many soldiers were getting frostbite from the cold winds on top of the tanks. There'd be no rest tomorrow, which was Christmas. The paratroopers in Bastogne had to be relieved.

Captain Anderson heard the sound of a vehicle approaching. He flicked off his flashlight, threw off the poncho, and saw a jeep with two stars painted on the fender heading toward him. Anderson stood because he knew it was the jeep belonging to General Barton Hughes, the division commander.

The jeep stopped a few feet away, and Hughes, wearing a parka with a fur collar, stepped out. Anderson marched toward him and saluted.

"Captain Anderson," said Hughes, "General Patton thinks we're not moving quickly enough, so I'm going to ride with you on the spearhead tomorrow. We're going to get up an hour earlier than usual, and we're going to push like hell because we've received word that the people in Bastogne can't hold out much longer. Pass the word along to your men."

"Yes, sir."

Captain Anderson rushed off to pass the word to his platoon leaders, and General Hughes looked around for a suitable spot to pitch his tent. Patton had told him that if he didn't move faster, he would be relieved of command, and Hughes would rather have been shot than be relieved of command. Therefore, he was going to ride the point tomorrow and lead the Hammerheads into Bastogne personally.

Hughes could hear some soldiers nearby singing "Silent Night," but as far as he was concerned, it was just another night in the war. He puffed his pipe and waited impatiently for his staff to arrive with his tent.

NINETEEN

On Christmas day, Field Marshal Model put through a telephone call to General Jodl at Hitler's headquarters in the Eagle's Nest.

"Jodl," he said slowly, struggling to keep his voice under control, "you must convince the Fuehrer that the drive to Antwerp must be broken off at once."

Jodl was silent for a few moments, then he said, "The Fuehrer will never agree."

"If he knows what's happening here, he'll have to agree,"

Model said. "The Allies have regrouped, received reinforcements, and are attacking all of my positions. Our offensive has come to a halt, and due to the tremendous losses we've taken, we no longer can conduct large scale operations. All we can do is pull back to a shorter defensive line and wait for reinforcements."

"There is nothing to reinforce you with," Jodl said. *"Wacht am Rhein* has already received everything we can spare. However, you cannot retreat. You must stand and fight."

"Can you send us more gasoline?"

"You were supposed to have sustained your attack with captured fuel."

"We've captured practically nothing. The Americans have blown everything up. Jodl, you must talk to the Fuehrer about this. We don't have much time to waste. Some of my divisions are in danger of being encircled even as we speak."

"I'll speak with him right away," Jodl replied. "In the meanwhile, you are not to retreat one millimeter. Is that clear?"

Jodl hung up the phone, badly shaken. He'd studied the reports and seen the dispositions, but until now nobody had actually said that *Wacht am Rhein* had failed. Some high-ranking officers, including Model, had said from the beginning that the offensive didn't have enough men, tanks, and gasoline to succeed, but the Fuehrer had insisted that it would succeed, and Jodl had believed him.

Now he had to tell Hitler the bad news, and Hitler didn't take bad news well. He'd rant and rave, and Jodl would have to sit still and put up with it. Jodl drummed his fingers on his desk for a few moments, trying to pull himself together for the task that lay ahead, and then stood, smoothed the front of his tunic, and set off for Hitler's office.

The closer the Hammerheads got to Bastogne, the stiffer the resistance became. They still were three miles away on Christmas night, and the next morning the Germans fought them to a complete standstill.

General Hughes directed the attack from the front, exposing himself to enemy fire continually and exhorting the

Hammerheads to push forward, but the Hammerheads could take no ground. There simply were too many German tanks out there. Finally, at ten o'clock in the morning, Hughes called General Patton and stated that he needed help. Hughes expected to be chewed out, but Patton only said that he'd send whatever he could.

Hughes hung up and looked over the top of his trench at the battlefield. A vast panorama of war was spread before his eyes. Tanks fought on the road and in the open fields, and infantry soldiers advanced against each other in the surrounding woods. Hughes felt certain that he could break through on the road if he had another ten or twenty tanks, but he'd already committed his reserves and didn't have anything left.

He hoped Patton would send help soon because he was afraid the Germans might breach his lines.

The battle seesawed back and forth for the rest of the morning and the early part of the afternoon. General Hughes shifted units constantly and probed for weaknesses in the German line, but he couldn't find anything. The field was littered with ruined German and American tanks, and a constant stream of ambulances carried the wounded to the field hospital a few miles back.

At three o'clock in the afternoon, an aide told Hughes that tank reinforcements were on the way from the rear. Twenty minutes later they arrived, twenty medium tanks covered with ice and muck. They stopped nearby, and a husky cigar-smoking man climbed down from the lead tank.

Hughes walked toward the lead tank, and saw that the cigar-smoking man was a colonel with rugged lumpy features. The colonel took one look at General Hughes's stars, drew himself to attention, and saluted.

"Colonel Creighton Abrams reporting, sir," the man said.

Hughes returned the salute. "Good to see you, Abrams. I want you to lead us into Bastogne."

"Yes, sir!" Abrams replied.

Hughes returned to his radio and organized the attack. The tanks in the field below would protect Abrams's flanks, and Abrams would try to bull his way through the road. A battalion of infantry would follow on trucks in case foot soldiers were needed, and he decided to send the first battalion of the Fifteenth Regiment, which was fighting in the woods nearby.

Captain Anderson received the order over his field radio and gradually moved his men back squad by squad so that Baker Company on the left and Dog Company on the right could cover his positions. When his company was withdrawn, he marched the men out of the woods and up the hill to the division's command post.

Colonel Simmons met them and told them to load onto the trucks lined up behind the tanks from the Fourth Armored Division.

General Hughes stood near Colonel Abrams's tank. The word was passed forward that everything was in readiness, and General Hughes raised his arm in the air and pointed it toward Bastogne.

"MOVE 'EM OUT!" he yelled.

The tanks revved their engines and rolled down the hill. The German tanks in the fields saw them coming but were too heavily engaged to do anything about them. In the lead tank, Colonel Abrams told his gunner to use the cannon to keep the road clear.

The tank drivers brought their big lumbering vehicles to top speed. A German tank rumbled onto the road in front of them, and Abrams's gunner fired on it immediately. The shell streaked forward and scored a direct hit, blowing the German tank off the road and onto its side.

The Combat Command roared down the road, followed by Charlie Company in trucks. Shells exploded all around the road, and bullets whizzed through the air. In the fourth truck from the front, Cranepool and his men hugged the floor and squirmed to get lower, as bullets whammed into the fenders of the truck.

A German shell hit one of the American tanks, and the tank behind it pushed it off the road and kept going. American artillery on the hill behind them redoubled their efforts to cover the column, and more German tanks were transformed into blazing funeral pyres.

The German commander in the woods below, seeing the American tank force breaking through, feared encirclement.

He immediately ordered that his men fall back and reorganize to meet that threat.

On the American hill, General Hughes studied the battlefield through his binoculars and perceived, through the smoke, that the Germans were pulling back.

"We've got them on the run boys!" he shouted. "Now go after them! CHARGE!"

The tanks and trucks sped along the road to Bastogne. They passed forests and fields, crossed a bridge that the Germans had neglected to blow, and didn't even bother to slow down for a few platoons of German infantry that fired at them.

They barreled down a hill, crossed a valley, and then at the foot of the next hill, an artillery piece fired in front of them, and one of the American tanks was blasted to smithereens.

General Abrams realized it probably was an 88 straight ahead up the hill, and he'd have to send the infantry up to knock it out. He ordered his tanks off the road and told them to disperse and then radioed Captain Anderson of Charlie Company, telling him to lead his men through the woods and put the 88 out of action.

The trucks rumbled into the field and hid behind some trees. Captain Anderson ordered the men to unload, formed the first three platoons into a column of twos, and ordered his heavy weapons platoon to lob mortar rounds up the hill at the 88.

The first platoon took the point, and Lieutenant Woodward led it up the hill. Not far behind him, Cranepool trudged beside the medic, Pfc Grossberger, and heard the first of the mortar rounds go *pop* behind him as they were fired at the artillery emplacement.

The hill became steeper, and the men had to pull themselves up by holding onto the branches of trees. A few of them fell and toppled backwards for ten or twenty feet, but Lieutenant Woodward was surefooted as a mountain goat, and had no patience with the men who couldn't move as quickly as he.

"What's the matter with you guys?" he chided. "You're like a bunch of old women!"

Cranepool had come to dislike Woodward considerably, and several times during the past few days, he'd thought about putting a bullet through Woodward's head. Cranepool knew that if Mahoney had been around, the sparks really would fly. Mahoney couldn't tolerate arrogant officers, but he usually handled them pretty well because he generally knew more than they did.

The big German 88 fired again, and the men from the first platoon could see its smoke up ahead.

"There it is!" said Corporal Fanucchi, pointing up the hill.

"Keep your voice down!" replied Lieutenant Woodward. "Skirmish line!"

The first platoon formed a skirmish line, and the second platoon did the same on the first platoon's right flank. Captain Anderson held the third platoon in reserve, while his fourth platoon, which was his weapons platoon, lobbed mortar rounds at the 88, without having much effect from what Cranepool could see.

Lieutenant Woodward signaled to Captain Anderson, and Captain Anderson radioed the mortar squads, telling them to stop firing. Seconds later the woods became quiet.

Captain Anderson spoke to Lieutenant Woodward. "Move 'em in," he said.

Lieutenant Woodward raised his carbine in the air and shouted, "LET'S GO, MEN! FOLLOW ME!"

He ran up the hill, holding his carbine at port arms, and the rest of the platoon followed him. To the right, SFC Frank Guffey led the second platoon forward. The men shouted battle cries and whooped it up to give themselves courage and scare the Germans.

Cranepool peered through the branches ahead and saw the gray sandbags that surrounded the 88.

"We're almost there, men!" Lieutenant Woodward yelled. "Let's go!"

Cranepool tripped on a piece of ice and fell on his face, just as he heard a loud burst of machine gun fire to his front. Men around him screamed, and he turned to see blood spurt from the chest of Pfc Finch.

"HIT IT!" screamed Lieutenant Woodward.

He dived on to the snow, but his order was unnecessary because all of his men had dived for shelter as soon as they had heard the machine gun fire. Some of them didn't make it, and their blood dribbled over the snow.

They were pinned down by two machine guns in the German artillery emplacement. Cranepool looked up the hill and saw the flashes coming from their barrels. If Mahoney had been there, he would've had a plan figured out already for silencing the machine guns, but Lieutenant Woodward thought he'd better get some advice from Captain Anderson.

"Sir—we can't move!" he said excitedly.

"Try to move your platoon around the emplacement and take it from behind. I'll cover you with the second and third platoon."

Captain Anderson handed the walkie-talkie to his runner and looked at the artillery emplacement. "All right men—come with me!"

He crawled to the left, and the first platoon followed him. They cradled their rifles in their arms and kept their heads low as they slithered over the snow. They made their way around the emplacement and gradually approached it from the rear. Lieutenant Woodward gathered his squad leaders and told them that the first and second squads would move close enough to throw hand grenades, and the third and fourth squads would provide cover in case any Germans showed their heads. He would stay back with the third and fourth squads to direct the operation.

Cranepool returned to his squad, told them what to do, and when Lieutenant Woodward gave the signal, he moved them forward. They crawled through the underbrush and around trees toward the artillery emplacement. Cranepool's knees had become frigid due to constant contact with frozen snow. He crawled over a snow covered log, all the while keeping his eyes riveted on the artillery emplacement, and he thought that in about twenty more yards they'd be able to get off some grenades.

A shot rang out, and he saw a puff of smoke coming from the sandbags up ahead. The bullet zipped into the snow a few feet from Private Parker, and they all stopped cold, trying to burrow lower into the snow. More single shots were fired, and Cranepool realized that the Germans had expected an attack from their rear and posted a few riflemen to cover it.

"Gimme some BAR fire!" Cranepool yelled.

His two BAR men jammed rounds into the chambers of their automatic weapons and opened fire on the rear of the bunker. The Germans stopped shooting their rifles as they ducked to avoid the bullets.

Cranepool pulled a grenade from his lapel and jumped to his feet. "LET'S GO!" he screamed.

He yanked the pin and ran with his arm back toward the artillery emplacement. The men in his squad followed him, also with hand grenades ready, and the BAR men kept firing, preventing the Germans from taking careful aim at Cranepool and his men.

A German hand grenade came flying out of the emplacement, and Cranepool jumped up, catching it in midair with his left hand. He dropped to the ground, threw the German hand grenade back into the emplacement, and then lobbed his own grenade in. He dived to the snow as his men threw their grenades and followed him down.

The grenades exploded one after the other, and the artillery emplacement became enveloped in smoke. Cranepool waited a few seconds, then jumped to his feet and charged.

"Up and at 'em!" he hollered.

He and his men ran toward the emplacement, which was now silent and shrouded with smoke. Behind them came Lieutenant Woodward and the second squad. The rest of Charlie Company attacked from the front. Cranepool jumped up onto the wall of sandbags and dropped into the emplacement, holding his carbine ready and peering through the smoke for movement and danger.

Mutilated Germans lay everywhere, and the sandbags were splashed with blood. The huge artillery piece was in the middle of the emplacement, and on the other side, American soldiers jumped down on dazed and bleeding Germans. Some of the Germans hadn't been wounded, but they knew they were licked and raised their hands in surrender.

Lieutenant Woodward arrived in the emplacement and appeared satisfied. He kicked a few Germans onto their backs, and found the captain who'd commanded the artillery crew sprawled dead over its rear sight. Woodward took the dead officer's pistol, looked at it, smiled, and jammed it into his belt.

Captain Anderson came around from the other side, holding his .45 in his right hand. "Any prisoners back here?"

"No, sir," said Woodward.

"All right. Let's get back to the trucks."

They climbed out of the artillery emplacement, taking their prisoners with them. Cranepool realized he had to take a piss, and paused to unbutton his fly. Suddenly he heard a sound. He grabbed his rifle and screamed: "HIT IT!"

Everybody scrambled to the snow, and Cranepool looked north into the woods.

"What is it!" demanded Lieutenant Woodward.

"I heard something in those woods over there."

"Where?"

Cranepool pointed with his carbine. "There."

Lieutenant Woodward raised his binoculars, and focused them on the spot Cranepool had indicated. He saw movement in the woods, and two men in American Army uniforms emerged.

"Hello over there!" one of them shouted. "What outfit are you with?"

"Third Army!" replied Woodward.

"THIRD ARMY!"

More American soldiers emerged from the woods, jumping up and down and shouting happily.

"THE THIRD ARMY IS HERE! WE'RE RELIEVED!"

They ran toward Charlie Company, holding out their arms. Cranepool got to his feet and saw a soldier with the patch of the Screaming Eagles on his shoulder. Cranepool didn't think he'd ever seen such joy on a man's face. The soldier grabbed Cranepool's hand and pumped it wildly.

Cranepool struggled to keep his balance. "Are you from Bastogne?" he asked.

"You're goddamned right!" the soldier replied, pointing behind him. "Bastogne is just on the other side of those trees there! And it's about time you fucking guys got here!"

TWENTY

In a little hotel that had not been damaged too badly by the fighting in Bastogne, Mahoney and Madeleine lay naked underneath a dozen blankets, kissing and writhing against each other, feasting on each other's bodies.

They'd been doing this ever since Christmas Eve. She had had to report to the hospital from time to time, and he'd made a few appearances at General McAuliffe's headquarters, but they'd spent most of their time in this dingy, little, unheated room, eating C rations and making love.

Mahoney was surprised by the depth of feeling he had for the little ex-whore. Instead of becoming tired of her, as he did with most women, he found the enchantment becoming stronger. He tried not to dwell upon what might happen in days to come because he was certain he'd be killed when the Germans resumed operations against Bastogne. In fact, he couldn't understand why it was so quiet today. He didn't know that many Germans soldiers who'd surrounded the city had been siphoned away to fight the threat coming from Patton's Third Army in the south.

They made love langorously, moaning and sighing, making little motions and kissing softly. It was the kind of lovemaking they did for hours on end, devoid of anxiety, two souls intermingling and at peace.

Through the pleasure and lazy sensuality, Mahoney became aware of a commotion in the street below. He raised his head and perked up his ears. "What the hell is that?"

She gazed at him, her cheeks flushed and eyes sultry. "What're you talking about?"

"Something's going on down there!"

Mahoney jumped out of bed, threw on his field jacket, and dashed to the window, opening it up and looking down into the streets below. He saw paratroopers running through the streets, screaming and waving their rifles in the air.

"HEY!" Mahoney shouted. "WHAT THE HELL'S GOING ON?"

A paratrooper looked up at him, and his face was crazed with delight. "THE THIRD ARMY IS HERE!"

"Holy shit!" Mahoney said.

"What is it?" asked Madeleine.

"We're not surrounded anymore!"

She got out of bed, wrapped herself in a blanket, and stood at the window beside Mahoney. They looked down and saw paratroopers and civilians pouring through the streets, heading toward the southern part of the city. They cheered and shouted, shook hands and passed bottles of wine around, as joy and celebration descended on Bastogne.

"Here they come," said Mahoney, pointing toward the south.

They leaned out the window and saw the tanks of the Fourth Armored Division rumbling down the street. Children ran beside the tanks and screamed happily. Their parents applauded, and some of them cried, overcome by the emotion of the moment. The paratroopers from the 101st Airborne jumped up and down and cheered.

Colonel Creighton Abrams stood in the turret of the lead tank, grinning and holding up his hands, making victory signs with his fingers while the news was flashed around the world that bloody Bastogne had been saved.

Read the Sergeant's next daring adventure

THE SERGEANT

HAMMERHEAD
BY GORDON DAVIS

Hitler's *Wacht am Rhein* offensive has given Germany a new opportunity to win the war in the west. Now all of the forces in Ardennes are coiled and ready to strike on Bastogne in an effort to crush the Allied forces. Meanwhile, General Patton has orchestrated an attack of his own designed to widen the Allies' narrow corridor into Bastogne from the south. If Patton does not succeed, the war could rage on indefinitely.

Sergeant C.J. Mahoney, back from temporary duty, is reunited with Charlie Company and walks smack into the face of the bloody confrontation. And he's got another battle in his own battalion—as a hard-nosed Lieutenant from West Point determines to strangle his authority and chop Mahoney down in front of his own men.

(#20118-2 • $2.25)

Read HAMMERHEAD, on sale December 15, 1981 wherever Bantam Books are sold or order directly from Bantam by including $1.00 for postage and handling and sending a check to Bantam Books, Dept. SA9, 414 East Golf Road, Des Plaines, Illinois 60016. Allow 4–6 weeks for delivery. This offer expires 6/82.

A towering novel of friendship, betrayal and love

THE LORDS OF DISCIPLINE

**by Pat Conroy
author of The Great Santini**

This powerful and passionate novel is the story of four cadets who become bloodbrothers. Together they will encounter the hell of hazing and the rabid, raunchy and dangerously secretive atmosphere of an arrogant and proud military institute. Together, they will brace themselves for the brutal transition to manhood... and one will not survive.

Pat Conroy sweeps you dramatically into the turbulent world of these four friends—and draws you deep into the heart of his rebellious hero, Will McLean, an outsider forging his personal code of honor, who falls in love with Annie Kate, a mysterious and whimsical beauty who first appears to him one midnight in sunglasses and raincoat.

(#14716-1 • $3.75)

Read THE LORDS OF DISCIPLINE, on sale January 15, 1982, wherever Bantam Books are sold or order directly from Bantam by including $1.00 for postage and handling and sending a check to Bantam Books, Dept. LD, 414 East Golf Road, Des Plaines, Illinois 60016. Allow 4–6 weeks for delivery. This offer expires 6/82.

THE SERGEANT

C.J. Mahoney—The Sergeant—a rough, tough guy, once a street kid from New York but now a damned good soldier who'll take on any dangerous mission handed him. Now you can follow Mahoney on his daring exploits in the skirmishes and major battles of World War II in all these action-packed books by Gordon Davis.

☐ 14708 THE LIBERATION OF PARIS #4 $2.25

☐ 14721 DOOM RIVER #5 $2.25

☐ 14712 SLAUGHTER CITY #6 $2.25

☐ 14895 BULLET BRIDGE #7 $2.25

☐ 20034 BLOODY BASTOGNE #8 $2.25

Buy them at your local bookstore or use this handy coupon:

Bantam Books, Inc., Dept. SR, 414 East Golf Road, Des Plaines, Ill. 60016
Please send me the books I have checked below. I am enclosing $_____
(please add $1.00 to cover postage and handling). Send check or money order
—no cash or C.O.D.'s please.

Mr/Mrs/Miss_____

Address_____

City_____ State/Zip_____

SR—11/81

Please allow four to six weeks for delivery. This offer expires 4/82.

SAVE $2.00 ON YOUR NEXT BOOK ORDER!
BANTAM BOOKS
Shop-at-Home Catalog

Now you can have a complete, up-to-date catalog of Bantam's inventory of over 1,600 titles—including hard-to-find books.

And, you can save $2.00 on your next order by taking advantage of the money-saving coupon you'll find in this illustrated catalog. Choose from fiction and non-fiction titles, including mysteries, historical novels, westerns, cookbooks, romances, biographies, family living, health, and more. You'll find a description of most titles. Arranged by categories, the catalog makes it easy to find your favorite books and authors and to discover new ones.

So don't delay—send for this shop-at-home catalog and save money on your next book order.

Just send us your name and address and 50¢ to defray postage and handling costs.

BANTAM BOOKS, INC.
Dept. FC, 414 East Golf Road, Des Plaines, Ill. 60016

Mr./Mrs./Miss_____
(please print)
Address_____
City_____ State_____ Zip_____

Do you know someone who enjoys books? Just give us their names and addresses and we'll send them a catalog too at no extra cost!

Mr./Mrs./Miss_____
Address_____
City_____ State_____ Zip_____

Mr./Mrs./Miss_____
Address_____
City_____ State_____ Zip_____

FC—9/81